a different kind of heat

ANTONIO PAGLIARULO

a different kind of heat

DELACORTE PRESS

Published by Delacorte Press
an imprint of Random House Children's Books
a division of Random House, Inc.
New York

Visit us on the Web! www.randomhouse.com/teens
Educators and librarians, for a variety of teaching tools, visit us at
www.randomhouse.com/teachers

Library of Congress Cataloging-in-Publication Data

Pagliarulo, Antonio.
A different kind of heat / Antonio Pagliarulo. — 1st ed.
p.   cm.
Summary: Trying to come to terms with her brother's death, high school
student and former gang member Luz meets his killer face to face as she
begins to rebuild her own life in a group home in New York City.
ISBN-13: 978-0-385-90319-6 (glb) — ISBN-13: 978-0-385-73298-7 (trade pbk.)
ISBN-10: 0-385-90319-7 (glb) — ISBN-10: 0-385-73298-8 (trade pbk.)
[1. Puerto Ricans—Fiction.   2. Brothers and sisters—Fiction.
3. New York (N.Y.)—Fiction.]   I. Title.
PZ7.P148Dif 2006
[Fic]—dc22
2005032170

The text of this book is set in 12-point Baskerville BE Regular.

Book design by Angela Carlino

Printed in the United States of America

May 2006

10 9 8 7 6 5 4 3 2 1

BVG

FOR MY MOTHER,
WITH LOVE AND THANKS

they say my name is Heartbreak
a girl who cries in the street—
they think I hide in the shadows
unable to accept defeat—
but what do they know about fighting
when they're not part of the war?
how can they see the dying
when they've never been at death's door?

I think my name is Danger
because I know what it means to bleed—
I've pulled the trigger and held the blade
and wrestled the violent need—
don't talk about teaching me lessons
'cause there ain't no more to learn
so walk away and watch your step
and let my little rage burn

1/3

SHOTS RANG OUT.

I woke to sirens and flashes of blue light. Now, as I write this, I can hear voices drifting up from the street—cops talking in code, a bystander giving his witness statement. I just glanced out the window and saw the medical examiner's truck round the corner. Must've been a drive-by.

The wind is blowing hard. The moon is full. It's a country chill, like the ones that hit those small towns upstate. Lately that image has been playing in my mind a lot. Acres of green land, a shingled house tucked behind a bunch of trees. I was walking down Broadway last week when it flashed in front of me. The buildings became cornstalks and the traffic disappeared. Almost got flattened by a bus because I was dreaming stupid dreams. But it feels good to think of a place far away.

This morning, Sister Ellen came up to me after breakfast and said, "Luz, do you know what today is?"

I shrugged. A holiday? A holy day? I didn't know.

She laughed and reminded me that a full year had passed since I first came to the St. Therese Home for Boys and Girls. It's my anniversary: 365 days of routine, 52 weeks of progress. She handed me this journal, a nice little gift, and suggested that I start writing. She explained in her usual cool way that words are like therapy. There's a rhythm to them, she said, that brings peace to the mind. Like when she kneels in the chapel and prays the rosary, one bead after another. Or like in the music that plays throughout the building at dusk–the "Salve Regina," I think it's called. Sounds like chanting.

I looked up at her, confused. We stood in the kitchen, just the two of us. You wouldn't believe she's almost fifty. The smooth white skin, the reddish hair, the dimples in her cheeks. I asked her if there was something specific she wanted me to write, if she'd be checking it like an assignment.

"No, of course not," she answered. "It's a journal, for your private use. You've been with us for an entire year and you've made wonderful improvements. Think about that. Write about it. It's for you and no one else."

So here I am, thinking. That's not always a good thing. The more I think, the more I come to believe that something's wrong with me, that I'm fucked up deeper than anyone knows. I mean, I'm probably the only seventeen-year-old in New York who's counting the days till vacation is over and school starts up again. Normal? No. I'll be graduating (hopefully) in June, so maybe it's just the anticipation that's wiring me up. But it's also the fact that I like keeping busy. I don't come home to a family anymore and I guess the loneliness is tougher than I want to believe.

A year. So many changes. Where do I begin?

Well, at the *beginning,* I guess. . . .

It's funny how I used to call this little bedroom a private prison. I remember my first day here, walking in and looking around and seeing only a desk, a bed, a bureau and a tiny round mirror on the wall. I was like: *Where's the phone? Where's the radio?* I spent the next few nights lying on my back listening to the traffic. I heard horns honking, people yelling, dogs barking. It didn't seem like a "home" to me. But I had no place to go.

That's what my probation officer said. That's what the judge said.

No place to go.

I never thought I'd get used to it here. The routine, I mean. Up in the morning. Take the train to school. Come back, do homework and chores and other bullshit. One hour of "recreation" a day. Still can't believe I made it a year.

Sometimes I think about what life was like before I came to St. Therese, and the picture ain't pretty. The fighting, the riots, cruisin' with my girls from Castle Hill and knocking over all those stores back in the Bronx. One thing led to another, I guess. What cracks me up is that I never got caught when I was a member of the crew. I did so much shit and not one single time did a cop pull me over or bring me in to juvenile hall. And then I start up with politics and find myself a ward of the state. Well, not "politics" exactly. I guess it was more like *protests*. But I don't want to get into that right now.

No, wait. That's wrong. I keep putting it off and I know I can't go on like this. It's like Sister Ellen says—you have to make peace with the past before sorting out the future. But how do I make peace with images of blood and a broken body? How do I make peace with *murder*?

Now it's done. I wrote the words. I opened up the doors. His face is floating like a vision before my eyes.

Julio, my heart. If you can hear me right now, if you're looking over my shoulder, you know how hard it is for me to be writing this. You can see the tears spilling from my eyes and dotting these pages.

Killed like that. On the street in the chill black of night. Did you look into the cop's eyes as he lifted the gun and fired? Did he say anything?

I'm taking deep breaths, trying to stop my heart from beating so fast. This always happens when I think about Julio. He was my brother, my guardian angel, the person I loved most. All of eighteen the day we put him in the ground. I haven't set eyes on a picture of him in at least six months, but I'll never forget his curly black hair and gray eyes. His sweet smile. People always said we looked alike.

Julio's death was my downfall, I guess you'd say.

4

I never talk about what happened that night, but I can't *stop* talking about Mickey Pesaturo, the cop who took my brother's life. He lives. He goes on. He was never even punished. Justified force is what the law called Julio's murder. But how can any murder be justified?

I asked Judge Conner that very question at my sentencing, the day before I was sent to live here at St. Therese. Standing there in a packed courtroom. Reporters writing down my every word. The old guy looked at me and started talking about the riot I had sparked a week earlier in front of city hall. Yeah, there was a fire. Yeah, a bunch of cops and civilians got hurt. But what did that have to do with *my* pain? Judge Conner told me in a stern voice: "Honoring the dead has nothing to do with harming the living, Ms. Cordero."

It's taken me a year to understand what he meant.

But it's still inside me, that little rage, that need to avenge Julio's death. I can hear it hissing. I haven't arranged or even attended a protest since coming here. I haven't done much of anything.

Thinking about it now, I'm not sure I agree with Sister Ellen—that I've made progress, that I've *changed*. Does a person really change when she's *forced* to? I read something about conformity last term in English class. The rules are being shaped and you're bending with them just 'cause you have to, but deep down inside nothing moves at all. Everything stays the same, like a block of cement or steel. It can't be sculpted. Maybe you can chisel away at the edges to make it prettier, but at the core it's always gonna be stiff and stubborn and immovable.

Shit. Can't think about it anymore.

Trying to be positive. . . .

So here's my list, the ways in which I've "changed":

- Cut down on my cursing
- Cut down on smoking (cigarettes). STOPPED smoking (blunts).
- No more drinking! (most of the time)
- Very few late nights (partying, hanging out, freaking out)
- Haven't attended/organized a protest
- Haven't gotten a tattoo or piercing . . . yet

Not too bad. I'm even being harsh, because I haven't snagged a cigarette in four days.

Just glanced out the window again. Three more police cruisers pulled up to the curb, sealing off the street. Definitely a drive-by. That's the third one this month.

Well, it's late. Time to catch some sleep, Luz.

That's funny. In Spanish my name means "light."

Why the hell am I so dark?

I LIKE TO think of myself as a veteran at St. Therese. I'm second-in-command. There are four of us living here. The little building attached to the church is our home. You can see it if you walk down 126th Street, over by Malcolm X Boulevard: a squat brick structure with barred windows and a cross on the door. Inside, it looks like a regular house. Kitchen, living room, two bathrooms. Statues decorate the walls. You can't go five feet without shaking hands with the Virgin Mary.

Bram Shelby has called this place home for two years. The day I arrived, he was standing in the hallway playing a violin. At first I didn't know what to think of him. Tall and gangly, with Chinese eyes and dark skin. His dreadlocks long and tinged with wisps of blond. Freckles across his cheeks. On the streets, he's what we call funky freak: you glance at him and then have to stare because you don't know if you're seeing black or white. His is the kind of face that's so bizarre it turns beautiful before your eyes.

That day, I put down my bag of clothes and stammered, not knowing what to say. He caught my confusion. Cracked a smile and said, "What's the matter? Never seen a yellow nigga?"

I laughed. And no—I'd never seen anyone like him. Or known anyone like him. I thought I had it rough because my brother was dead and our mother was upstate serving time, but then Bram told me his story. Put up for adoption when he was just a baby. Went from one foster home to another. He ran away twenty times before moving to St. Therese. Bram didn't belong to a gang like me. He got by stealing and dealing, served a little time at juvie. The most amazing thing, though, is the way he plays that violin. That's how he makes money these days. After school and on weekends, he performs in the subway, usually at Grand Central and sometimes at Times Square. Lately he's been writing lyrics too. It's cool shit.

Martin Bloss got here four months after I did. Marty's a stunner too, but not in the same way as Bram. Marty reminds me of those models you see on the covers of magazines. He's got blond hair and blue eyes and the hottest body this side of the Atlantic. A white boy if ever there was one. Even talks like a yuppie, like he's from the Upper East Side or the suburbs. I call him The Party because he's always ready to sneak out after curfew and hit the clubs. But that's Marty's problem—he gets high too much. Put anything in front of him and he'll smoke it. He's into ecstasy and K and that shit that gives you hallucinations. Sad story. I know he has a hard time dealing with his own issues. He's been with a lot of girls, but

Marty likes guys too. Not that I care—I don't. Just hope he's careful about where he's plugging it in.

And then there's Clare. Quiet Ms. Santoro is what I call her. She's been here for three months. I don't know much about her except that she doesn't like talking and is covered with piercings. Girl's got more holes than a golf course. A little heavy, with buzzed hair and smooth white skin. It takes a lot to make her smile. Fifteen but she looks a lot older. At our weekly group therapy sessions, it's Clare who has to be forced to speak. She doesn't open up that easily. Strange, because she's not shy about undressing in front of me. We'll be talking in her room and suddenly she'll yank off her clothes and reach for her pajamas or sweats. She has scars. Too many. I can't bring myself to ask her how she got them.

I don't consider Sister Ellen one of us, but she's the only rock of strength we know. She's the foundation, as Bram likes to say. When I first got to St. Therese, I didn't wanna talk about anything—not my mother, not Julio and definitely not myself. But Sister Ellen knew how to get past my steel wall. She started out by telling me all about herself. She grew up in the Midwest, then came to New York after college. She went on to become a psychologist and worked in hospitals for a long time. Thirty years old when she got the "calling." She became a nun, a sister of St. Therese of the Holy Face, and was sent here to manage the outreach program for troubled youth. I look at her and see a religious person. Truth is, she's pretty cool. I've heard her curse in the kitchen while making dinner, and I know she had a boyfriend when she was twenty-five.

This afternoon, she led the group therapy session in the living room. It works like this: she gives us a topic, and then one by one we voice our opinions on it. Could be anything. Today, Sister Ellen brought up the issue of safety because of the other night's drive-by shooting at the corner. A drug-related crime, we were told, and a twenty-eight-year-old man was killed. Things like this scare Sister Ellen. She was shaken up, wringing her hands and shaking her head a lot.

"How does this make all of you feel?" she asked. "Is there anything we should do about it?"

So the five of us sat there, slumped against the couch, thinking about it. All I needed—the image of a man bleeding on the sidewalk. Like I hadn't been through that before.

It was Marty who spoke first. Raising his hands in that crazy animated way, the words shooting out of him. Saying, "Well I mean it's a terrible tragedy and all but it's over and done with and I hope the victim didn't suffer all that much, ya know?"

Sister Ellen asked him if it made him feel scared.

Marty thought about it. Then he said it sort of scares him, especially the thought of being hit by a stray bullet. That's what happened in the projects last week. Happens in the projects every damn week.

But Bram cut in right away. "That wouldn't have happened," he snapped. He kept his eyes centered on the floor, like always. "This was a drug-related crime and dealers know their targets. They aren't sloppy when they commit crimes. That's how come they get so far, and so wealthy. It's not like it is with gangs, who just drive by and spray bullets for a few rounds, hoping to hit their man. Dealers are *precise*."

We all got quiet. He was right. That's how it is on the streets, in the inner city. If you've lived here, you know the language. You know the rhythm of the night and the pulse of frightened hearts. The violence becomes just another thing to deal with.

Sister Ellen didn't like his comment. She asked him if we're just supposed to ignore the random shootings because they're bound to happen again and again.

Bram shrugged like he didn't care. But I knew what he was thinking deep down. He's too smart not to be affected. But admitting that he sometimes gets scared would make him seem less macho. Why are guys like that?

Sister Ellen looked at Clare, who was tearing up pieces of her napkin. Clare was dressed in jeans and a stained T-shirt. There was a fresh scab on her arm, as if she had scraped up against something sharp. "It scares me," she said, then followed that with the usual minute of silence. "It makes me feel like I never wanna go outside again."

Bram said right away that she couldn't let that happen to herself. You can't live like a prisoner, he said, because when there's a war, you have to *fight*.

They started arguing and I tuned them out. I never got a chance to voice my opinion because the hour was up and we all had chores to do. I'm not really sure how the safety issue makes me feel anyway. I mean, a drive-by shooting is nothing new. Even back home in the Bronx, shit happened all the time. Long before Julio was shot, I would hear about the kids who got killed in gang fights or from drag racing or drug overdoses. Nothing you can do about it.

Anyway, Sister Ellen dropped a little bomb before the session let out. She thinks the escalating violence in our neighborhood is a big issue, so in a few weeks police officers from the street crimes unit are coming here to talk to us and give us lessons in self-defense.

Yeah. Okay. That'll work. Which one of us gets to hold the magic wand?

I think Sister Ellen should've talked to me about that first. She knows how I feel around cops. I can't look at one without seeing Mickey Pesaturo—or Julio. I see a cop and I think, *Blood*. I think of blood and my mind says, *Whose?* My mind starts asking questions and I know another sleepless night is ahead.

1/8

PICTURE THIS: YOU walk into a school that's already overcrowded and dirty and find out that classes are gonna start an hour late because five more teachers quit during the holiday break. The principal is telling students to relax and go to homeroom. But guess what? Every classroom is packed and there aren't any spare desks. So the ugly hallways become a waiting area. Freshmen, sophomores, juniors, seniors . . . all of us standing around doing nothing. Oh, yeah—I'm learning. It would be easier to stay in my room and watch the Discovery Channel all day.

It's Monday. Windy-cold outside. I'm sitting in the cafeteria trying not to think about Jackson High School and the five months I have left here. It stinks like spoiled milk and fish. My classes are boring. I mean, what's the point of statistics anyway? $X=$ bullshit squared. I haven't seen Bram at all. Clare is probably hiding out in the library again, nose buried in a book. I took the train with Marty this morning and it was anything but pleasant. So many crowds. Bodies slammed together, armpits in my face. The people with the biggest asses trying to squeeze into the smallest seats. A guy in a business suit kept crinkling his newspaper in front of me. I told him to stop, and when he didn't, I slapped my hand clear through the business section. It's gonna be a bad day. I have three more classes, and then it's on to my probation officer.

Right now, though, I'm worried about Marty. The kids here tease him a lot because he's so crazy and flashy. He came to school dressed in jeans, a black sweater and pink sneakers. Don't ask me where he got those. I've seen the thugs pick on him before, calling him faggot and queer and shit like that. If I were him, I'd have taken a blade to their eyes a long time ago. But Marty doesn't know how to defend himself. That's why he hates school so much. In a way, I don't blame him. But I have to look out for him. He's bound to get hurt one of these days and I can't let that happen. The dickheads who tease him, they wouldn't dare mess with me because everyone knows I was in a crew. I'll fuck them up, plain and simple.

Damn. Bell just rang. On to my next thrilling class.

6:45 P.M.

My probation officer is concerned. Her name is Anne Burns and she's been putting up with me for a while, ever since I attended my first protest against police brutality and ended up spending a couple of hours in jail.

Anne is pretty. She's short and thin and has curly red hair. About forty years old. Her office on Chambers Street looks like a mouse cage. Once a month, I have to report to her. She records my progress while I'm living at St. Therese, then sends her findings to child welfare and juvenile court. I was sentenced to three years probation. With good behavior and a little luck, the term could easily be reduced.

"So," Anne said, sitting back in her chair, "tell me what's new."

I did. Nothing's new.

"Are you passing all of your classes?"

"Yes." (No.)

She paused for a minute, scribbling something in her notebook. Then she looked up at me and just stared.

I waited, preparing for the worst. I knew that stare.

"Sister Ellen tells me that you've been surfing the Internet a lot these days. She said you spend a lot of time cruising through a site that lists all of the upcoming police protests. Is that true?"

My cheeks felt hot. That nun is always watching. Can she fly too? I told Anne I was looking, but that didn't mean I was planning on going to any.

She leaned forward in her chair and stared at me. "Listen, Luz. You've made progress, but you know the rules. If you're caught attending one of these protests again, the courts could move to throw you in jail. You're not too young to be tried as an adult."

"There's nothing wrong with wanting justice." I didn't wanna say it, but the words just slipped out.

Anne sighed. "And what about the people who want justice to come and pay *you* a visit? What about them? They were protesting peacefully in front of city hall when you decided to turn it into a riot. Do you remember that?"

Yeah, I remember.

"You grabbed a megaphone and screamed at them to take back the streets, to rail against a police state. Do you remember that?"

I remember.

"You chucked glass bottles into the air, three of which hit and hospitalized innocent bystanders, and then you lit a fire that consumed two police cruisers. Do you remember that?"

I remember.

"You resisted arrest and actually *bit* the police officers who held you down. Do you remember that?"

I remember, bitch. Now leave me alone.

But she didn't. She went through the drill, listing the charges against me: assault (levels A and C, felony), battery (misdemeanor) and conspiracy to deface private and public property (misdemeanor). Anne tells me all the time that the courts took pity on me, that anyone else—a black male, specifically— would've been locked up for a year or two in maximum security. Don't know if I believe her. I'm Latina. I'm Puerto Rican. I'm Hispanic. The way I see it, girls like me aren't considered *all-American*. I've met a few white people who're amazed that I'm seventeen and haven't popped out a baby yet.

I got up the nerve to ask Anne about Mickey Pesaturo, the cop who shot my brother. I already knew what the answer was gonna be, but some things you just have to ask, ya know? So I asked her if Mickey Pesaturo was still a cop.

She nodded. "Yes, Luz. He is. You know that. A grand jury cleared Mickey Pesaturo of any wrong-doing. Get it through your thick head."

I didn't look at her.

She said, "What else was the grand jury sup-posed to do, Luz? You swore under oath that you didn't witness Julio's shooting. That you only heard the shot and then found him lying on the ground. That you didn't see *anything* else—"

"I told the police the truth," I snapped, cutting her off. "What I saw is what I saw. But I know Mickey Pesaturo isn't an innocent cop."

"Save it," she said, holding up her hands.

Anne spent the rest of our time discussing my "rage issues." I had to speak to a few doctors before coming to St. Therese, and they all said that I needed anger management courses and more ag-gressive therapy. Maybe they were right. My temper is too hot, and it's what got me into trouble in the first place. Don't know why I'm like this. Certain things just set me off, I guess. My blood boils and my knuckles crack and I'm blind to consequence. If I think something's wrong, I'm gonna damn well make it right—no matter the cost.

It was like that last year, the afternoon I decided to turn city hall into an inferno. A Friday. Cold winds, thickening clouds. I had been attending protests and rallies since Julio's death, but this one was different. Here, I was the center of attention. People cheered as I emerged from the subway station, patting my shoulders and calling after me. *Luz, keep your head up! Hey, Luz, fight the good fight!* They'd seen me on the news two nights earlier, one of countless interviews. Cursing mouth, wide eyes. The girl with the bad attitude. Yeah, that was me.

I made it to the steps of city hall and looked around. Must've been a thousand people huddling together. They were holding up picket signs that read STOP KILLING OUR KIDS and BRUTALITY=MURDER! and INNOCENT BLOOD. Mothers brought pictures of their dead sons, young men from the inner city who had died as unnecessarily as my own brother. Even before the reporters arrived, tears were flowing.

And then the chanting started.

"No justice?"

"No peace!"

Someone hoisted me up, onto the hood of a parked car. The police were already moving in. I swept my eyes over them and saw a wall of blue: uniforms, helmets, nightsticks. Would they take out their guns and shoot me too? Standing there, high above it all. Looking down on *them*. I saw the same face over and over—the face of my enemy, Mickey Pesaturo. A hundred cops, but all the same cop.

I don't know who handed me the megaphone. It was in my hands and I was screaming, rousing the crowd, forcing them to rail against a society that wanted nothing other than oppression. It had already claimed too many victims. "Fight!" I remember screeching. "Take back your rights. Do it for your sons, your brothers! Do it *now!*"

And in the blink of an eye, the sky fell.

There were little explosions and loud cries. Glass shattered. The crowd became a wave. I jumped down onto the street and swung my fists at the first cop I saw. Smelled fear. Tasted blood. It was madness. I don't remember starting the fire. I mean, maybe I did, maybe there was kerosene in my hands and newspaper bunched in my jacket, but I never meant to hurt anyone. Not completely . . .

Anyway, got home about an hour ago. Tonight I'm on cooking duty, which means I have to help Sister Ellen chop vegetables and pound hamburgers. Fun, fun, fun. I'll try to get through it smiling.

9:32 P.M.

I tried. No smiles available tonight.

1/10

Dear Mom,

I know it's pointless for me to write a letter to you in my journal when I'll never mail it. Please forgive me. It's just that I can't stand scrawling those words onto the envelope underneath your name. CORRECTIONAL FACILITY. They make me feel so fucking sick. Is it really the way it's shown in the movies? I hate to think of it. Do you live in a tiny cell? Are the other women mean to you? Oh God, Mom—I remember how you always hated closed spaces and too much noise. When we lived in the Bronx above that candy store, you used to keep all the doors open because you were afraid they'd lock and seal us into that one tiny bedroom.

It's been a long time since I heard your voice. That's my fault because I haven't called or come up to visit. I just can't. Last year, right after I came to St. Therese, I got on the train and made it halfway up there before realizing that I couldn't handle it. I know you don't believe that— impossible that tough-as-nails Luz wouldn't be able to handle something, right? But in this case it's true. I guess it's easier for me to deal with *being alone than to deal with the fact that I won't be seeing you for at least another three years. I wasn't there the day they took you away. I have no memory of that. So for me it's as if you just disappeared, and right now that's what I can deal with.*

I can't even begin to describe what life is like now that Julio is gone. I relive his death every day but I can't talk about it. I can't even write about it. No one knows what really went down that night. Sometimes I think the memories and my fears and all the blood will drown me, but then I remember that I'm still breathing. That I have to go on. Things are pretty decent here at St. Therese, I guess. They tell me I've made changes for the better, and maybe it's true. I'm trying hard to get my act together.

I've gotten every one of your letters. I've read them. You don't have to keep explaining yourself to me—I know why you're locked up. I'm making my peace with it little by little. I still think you could've done other things to make ends meet, but now I understand that you had an addiction to the drugs you were selling. So in a way it wasn't all your fault. You weren't there a lot while I was growing up, so I try to remember the good times we had. There was that Christmas when we took the train to Rockefeller Center and drank hot chocolate close to the tree. One summer, we went to the beach a few times and that's why I know how to swim.

You always ask me if I have a boyfriend. Why is that so important to you? I mean, you had boyfriends coming in and out of our apartment all the time and they treated you like shit mostly. I did so much messing around when I was in the gang. One boyfriend after another. But it's not like that anymore. Everything that happened in the last year . . . it kind of took the feeling outta me. I don't think about guys as much as I used to. I don't think about warmth or love. It's just coldness around me.

One day, when you ask me why I never wrote to you, I'll show you these pages and you'll know that you never left my thoughts. We'll sit around my apartment, drink coffee and catch up. I believe that. But right now, this is all I can do. If you lived inside my head for just a single minute, you'd forgive me and understand why.

1/12

WE SHOULDN'T HAVE done it.

Me and Bram took the train to school this morning, but I knew from the look on his face that we weren't gonna be spending much time inside. Marty and Clare met us over by Washington Square Park. It was sunny and not too cold. I kept looking at my watch, thinking that I should've been sitting in English instead of on a bench in the Village. It's been a long time since I cut a day of school.

"What you guys wanna do?" Bram asked, puffing hard on a cigarette.

Everybody had suggestions except me. I was having an okay time just sitting there, looking around at the streets and the traffic, listening to planes drone overhead. Kept looking up at the sky, wondering where every jet was flying. California? Italy? Australia? It didn't matter. I'd give anything to be on one, going somewhere.

Bram hates it when I mention getting out of New York. The way he sees it, people who are born in the city have no right to leave. He also says they can never be happy anyplace else. I kind of understand that. The streets have blooded me. When my heart beats, it sounds like the 6 train roaring into the

Zerega Avenue station. It sounds like Grand Central at rush hour. Even my dreams are Technicolor: bright and wild as the lights blinking over Times Square, fast as the yellow cabs zooming through midtown. But there's still a part of me that wants silence—not necessarily the quiet you can *hear*. I mean more like the stillness of a barren place, where you can't be reminded of anything.

It was Marty who finally led us away from the park. He knew where to go. We took the train to Queens, to a shitty part of Astoria. I knew where we were headed once we stepped into the building and made our way into a dark and grimy basement. It was a morning party. A couple of kids Marty knows from school were cutting that day too and hosting a little event. I smelled the smoke and saw it hanging in the air before we even got to the room. Music was playing. The room was big and lit with a few candles. I saw a couple of familiar faces, said my hellos and then found a seat in a corner. Clare settled in next to me.

Marty knew almost everyone there. Maybe like fifteen people hanging out, drinking beer and lighting up. I guess it was a happy scene but I just couldn't get into it. I thought Bram would mind being there because he usually doesn't like crowds. Instead of complaining, he found a drink and started talking to some girl with big tits. Five minutes later they were making out on one of the broken couches. It wasn't my idea of a good time. I used to go to a lot of morning parties back in my old neighborhood, but now I feel like I've outgrown them. I'm not in with any of the cliques. The cheerleaders annoy me, and a lot of the other girls are just interested in hearing about my gang days. So I sat there and watched everyone else.

Nicky Johnson had weed. He's a senior, and he was selling fat blunts for five bucks a pop. Marty and Bram shared puffs, then passed a hit over to Clare. I didn't sample the merchandise. Haven't smoked weed in like a year and I promised that I'd stop completely, so it was a good test of will.

I saw Marty getting a little tight with Justin Smith, one of the star players of the school's basketball team. Makes me wonder if maybe Justin's into guys too. They were sitting real close together and they even disappeared for a while.

Getting back into the city was the worst. We had to make it home by three-thirty, but the trains were delayed all over Queens and Manhattan. Police activity at the Prince Street station. We sat together in the cramped car, and Bram and Marty kept checking each other's eyes to make sure they didn't look stoned. Sister Ellen once commented that she could easily spot a person on drugs because she grew up in the sixties. But Bram and Marty and Clare were okay. Actually, they seemed really relaxed, totally chilled. Almost happy.

✳ ✳ ✳

Bram just left my room. About an hour ago he walked around to the back of the building and climbed up the ivy wall to the second floor. Clawing at the glass like a cat. We're not allowed to hang out like that. The boys stay downstairs, the girls up here. Sister Ellen is still scared that we'll become attracted to each other and screw our brains out in the middle of the night. But that isn't gonna happen. No matter how often I tell her that I've come to think of Bram and Marty as my brothers, she won't budge on that rule.

We had a long talk, Bram and me. He's concerned. Said that I've been quiet lately and that today he saw a lot of fear in my eyes. I admitted to being scared. Then I asked him if he'd noticed a change in me in the last year.

He nodded. Told me that when I first came here I was a militant crazy girl who looked at everyone like they were enemies. I always talked about the cops and how much I wanted revenge. Shit like that. Now it's different. He thinks I've mellowed out.

Yeah, I know. I've become a weak little sap. I've never spoken to Bram about Julio, or what I saw the night he died. Bram said I should write about it. I had no idea that he wrote in a journal too, but he admitted it to me tonight. Said it's helped him sort out a lot of shit. He touched my heart like a little kid, telling me that sometimes he writes about what he

26

thinks his biological parents look like—a Chinese mother and a half-black, half-white father. Then he smiled that sad smile. I told him that maybe he'd find them one day, like they do on the reality TV shows. But he didn't buy it. He said if anyone wanted to find him, they already would have. He's probably right. What's a person supposed to feel when he knows he's not wanted, when he has no blood to call his own? I mean, my own mother fucked up a lot, but she always told me I was pretty. I know she was happy when I was born.

He changed the subject fast, asking me about my poems. He knows I've been writing a lot, so I showed him the verse I wrote last week. The original is scrawled on a sheet of notebook paper, stuffed under my mattress. I pulled it out and handed it to him. He read it out loud.

> *kids dying and mothers crying*
> *and my dreams are bright with pain,*
> *you deal and steal and spin the wheel*
> *but in the end it's all the same—*
> *music plays to the final dance*
> *and I don't stand a chance,*
> *so wipe your tears and forget your pity*
> *this is life in the inner city*

He looked up at me. "This is good shit," he said. "What else you got?"

But I didn't have the courage to show him some of the other stuff I've written. What would people think if they ever saw what goes through my head? We got quiet. And then, suddenly, he asked me about Marty. "You think he's gay?" Bram said.

Shock! Marty pretty much told me that he is. I mean, I know he's attracted to guys, but it's like our own little secret. I shrugged like I didn't know. Told Bram it didn't make any difference.

He agreed with me at first, then said he wasn't sure how he felt about it because he'd never known any gay guys. What gets Bram is the crazy way Marty acts sometimes, like he's looking for trouble. Like he doesn't care about all the abuse he gets.

But he cares. Names hurt. And I told Bram that, no matter what, Marty is one of us. Makes no difference who he kisses or fucks.

It was getting late, and I didn't feel like talking anymore. Bram left me a cigarette and then shinnied down the wall and back to his room.

I'm staring at the cigarette right now. Won't light it.

11:52 P.M.

Just lit it.

1/15

LAST NIGHT I dreamt of him. Woke up with his name on my mind and the memories playing in front of me.

This is how it was, and this is how it will never be:

Summer, the night before my fifteenth birthday. The Bronx was baking and another power outage had plunged the streets into darkness. No air-conditioning. No light. But outside, kids were playing on the sidewalk and running through the spew of an open fire hydrant. I had spent the day with my crew. Another sister was initiated, and we had to beat her in because she refused to get sexed in by the guys. My fists were sore. I had blood under my nails. Came home to an empty apartment and shut myself away from everything. I lit candles, killed a cockroach in the kitchen and waited for sunrise. Mom was out with one of her guys and I knew by eleven o'clock that she wouldn't be back till morning.

A few minutes later I heard the door open. Julio was standing there, smiling. His black hair hung down in front of his eyes. Dressed in jeans and a dirty white shirt. He looked older than sixteen from working too many hours at the deli, lifting boxes and crates and putting new Sheetrock on the walls. I hadn't seen him in a few days. He didn't always come home when he worked late.

He pressed a finger to his lips. "Be quiet," he said. "I don't want none of the neighbors to hear." He took me by the hand and led me out of the apartment. We walked down the shadowy hall, toward the door leading up to the rooftop. He pulled something out of his pocket and managed to pop the lock open. I was scared. The landlord had warned us that going up on the roof was forbidden. You could end up in a shelter for pissing off the landlord.

"Julio," I said, grabbing his shoulders. "We can't. What if–"

"Don't worry. I got your back, sweetie. Go ahead."

I climbed the stairs quietly and then pushed open the second door, stepping out onto the roof with a sigh. It was cool. So high up, we felt a little breeze and were able to see the buildings in Manhattan. The sky twinkled with lights. I turned and saw that Julio was cradling a brown paper bag. He kneeled on the ground, opened it. Out came two cupcakes and a can of beer. I didn't know what he was doing until I saw him slide a match into one of the cupcakes and light it.

He held it up. "Happy birthday, Luz."

I smiled and stared at the dancing flame.

"Come on," he said. "Make a wish!"

I shut my eyes. I took a breath. I wished for

everything in that single moment: a bigger apartment, a new air conditioner, more clothes, lots of money, a house in the suburbs. But a sudden wind came and snuffed the match out before I could do it.

Julio laughed. "You're not fast enough, Luz. You're thinking too much."

Yeah, that's always been my problem.

We sat down and ate the cupcakes. Julio opened the beer, drank it in big gulps. Past midnight, a little buzzed, he started asking me questions. Why wasn't I going to school? Why was I hanging out with that pack of girls, getting into cars and staying out late? I didn't answer him.

He said, "Look at me, Luz."

I did.

"I want you to be careful out there," he said. "The streets are rough, rougher than anything. You know what I'm talking about. The girls in your crew, so many of them already got kids of their own. I don't want you to end up like that. I'm doing what I have to do to help out around here, givin' Mom money and all that, but you gotta keep your head on straight. I'm busy workin' a lot."

I nodded, but I already knew too much. He had tattoos on his shoulders and scars from all the fights he'd gotten into. I saw the bulge in the pocket of his jeans and knew it was a switchblade. I'd asked him about it once but he told me never to ask about his business. He shelled out cash in the living room and helped put food on the table, so nothing else mattered. Life was life. That was our neighborhood. You learned not to ask questions.

I fell asleep on the roof, listening to the traffic from the street. When I woke up, Julio was gone. He had slipped a fifty-dollar bill in my pocket and vanished into the early morning.

1/17

NINE O'CLOCK. DARK and windy outside. Just finished using the computer in the living room, pretending to write an essay for English class. Instead I logged on and started surfing the Web. We're allowed to go online, but only when Sister Ellen grants us permission. I didn't feel like dealing with rules tonight. Guess I got a little twisted, in one of my curious moods, and figured that I'm old enough to do what the fuck I want some of the time.

I went back to the Street Fighters Web site and cruised all of the upcoming protests.

Last week, a twenty-year-old black guy named William Brown was hauled in to jail after a traffic stop in Brooklyn and something happened. Don't know if he resisted arrest or if the cops found something in his car, but he arrived at the precinct all banged up and bloodied. Lips cut. Eyes swollen shut. The site had a whole story about him. There were like a million posts from people, all of them about police brutality and how William should never have been beaten up. Of course, the cops involved said he became violent and they had to react.

I'm angry.

Restless.

Pissed off.

I mean, how come we never read about white men getting all fucked by the cops? It's always the blacks and the Puerto Ricans. I'm not trying to get all worked up. I'm not whining or ranting either. It's just that it scares me. And I've seen it at school too, the way the security guards look at me sometimes. Or the way they study the black kids. They don't narrow their eyes at Marty or Clare like that.

There's a protest happening tomorrow in Brooklyn, on the block of the precinct where William Brown was booked. It's mad crazy, but I'm itching to go. Am I still that nuts?

1/18

YES, I AM.

Cut last period today and found myself hiding out in the third-floor girls' bathroom. Confused. I had been thinking about the protest all day. Going meant trouble. But not going meant trouble too. I guess it's that I don't wanna face the possibility that I'm not so fearless anymore. I mean, who wants to look in the mirror and see a stranger?

I almost saw that today. Stood there against the sink, breathing hard. Heard my watch ticking the minutes away. I couldn't make myself move. And then all of a sudden the door swung open fast, the way it does when a teacher or security guard does a random check. But it was Clare. She was cutting her Spanish class, and we laughed finding each other there, holed up against the sinks and toilets. She took one look at me and knew something was wrong. I told her everything. How I felt. How I wanted to go to the protest.

"Okay then," she said in her quiet, easy way. "Let's go."

Guess I needed someone else's approval, because in minutes we were on the D train, headed for Brooklyn. Took twenty minutes. When we got out onto the street, I tied a bandanna around my head, stuffing most of my hair inside it, and slipped on a pair of old sunglasses. My hands were a little jittery. Kept looking around.

It was the same as always: the chanting on the wind, the crowds. We saw picket signs before we even made it to the block. But when we got to the corner, I stopped.

Clare asked me what was wrong.

Told her I needed a minute to collect myself. It felt like a panic attack, an invisible hand holding me back. We waited and smoked a cigarette. I didn't wanna face Clare just then because I wasn't sure what she was thinking of me. I listened as someone started shouting into a megaphone and cheers went up. Traffic ground to a halt. Cops came out of every nook, readying themselves for the worst.

"No justice?"

"No peace!"

The pictures started flowing through my head. It was too much. I didn't wanna be there. I was afraid someone would recognize me and let the word out. What if I saw one of my girls from the old neighborhood? What if I saw Mickey Pesaturo?

After another cigarette and another minute, Clare tugged on my arm. "Come on," she said. "Let's head back home."

I looked at her. Asked her what she meant.

And she said, "It's okay to admit it, Luz. You just

don't wanna do this." She stared beyond the corner, at the thickening crowd, and then back at me. She told me that it was old shit, a part of the past, and that I didn't belong there with the protesters anymore.

I hesitated for a second, angry. Told her I did. And that she just didn't understand where I was coming from.

"Why do you think that?" she shot back. "Because I'm white? Because I was never in a gang? I understand a lot of things. I might not talk a lot, but I can still think."

I asked her what she knew about cops and brutality and how people like me are treated. Heard my voice getting loud. Felt my anger boiling. Turned away so that she couldn't see my face.

Then Clare said, "My brother died in my arms too."

That got me. I looked at her. "What?"

"My brother died in my arms, Luz," she said. "He was only four, but it was still hard. He had AIDS."

Felt like I was blown back ten feet. Didn't know what to say.

Clare saw the question marks on my face. Her eyes were hard, squinting. Seemed like she was considering whether to say something else. Then the words fell from her lips. Her mother was a heroin addict, she told me. Bad smack. Clare hadn't even met the woman till she was thirteen, but by then her mother was sick with AIDS. She'd had Clare's little brother a few years before that. Now they're both gone. Clare said, "You'd be surprised, Luz. There're people in this world who've been through just as much as you."

Felt like a fucking moron. Stood there listening to the chanting, like an old song playing out of tune. Wanted to apologize but the words just didn't come.

Clare looked back down the street. She asked me if I was gonna hang around and kick a cop's ass.

That made me laugh. Told her that I couldn't help it sometimes, that when I thought about Julio, about how much I loved him and how much I lost, I got fired up. And that when I saw a cop I was reminded of all the little wars we were fighting in the inner city. How do you win? I threw a glance at the screaming crowd, but I just didn't feel anything for it. Not today. It was weird. Like I was part of the photograph but somehow missing from the picture.

We walked away from the protest and headed home. We didn't speak for much of the train ride. Instead we just sat there, huddled close together, listening to the screech of the wheels on the tracks.

5:18 P.M.

Just got back from Clare's room. Spent the last hour sitting on her bed, talking. I couldn't help it– her words today got to me. Felt like such an asshole after she told me about her little brother.

38

She opened up to me tonight. Stuff I never expected to hear.

Clare's white, and I have this stupid tendency to think white people don't have pain or know struggle. But she knows it like I do. Born into a bad home and to a teenage mother, Clare was put up for adoption when she was two but instead got passed around from one foster home to the next. Then, when she was thirteen, her mother came looking for her. It was already too late because the woman was sick with HIV. Clare found out she had a little brother, Owen. But her mother had him the same way she'd had Clare—by sleeping around, selling herself for drugs. Clare and Owen were both mistakes.

Clare hesitated after telling me all that, then reached under her bed and pulled out a shoe box. She had a snapshot of the boy, taken just before he died. Stringy blond hair, red pimples scarring his cheeks. There was a sickly color to him, a yellowish tint. You looked at him and knew he was sick.

I closed my eyes and handed the picture back to her.

She'd been lucky living in a foster home only three miles from the shelter where her mother and Owen were staying. Clare had two good months of getting to know the woman who'd given birth to her. She got to play with her little brother too.

Made me think of my own mother, sitting in a jail three hours away. Haven't heard her voice in so long.

Clare said her mother was a pretty woman, but by then her face and body had gone skeletal. They talked a lot during those two months. In the end, Clare decided not to blame her mother for anything. The woman had been the victim of a hopeless life. Needles and hot spoons were the only things she'd ever known.

The morning Clare's little brother died, she was at his bedside. She'd made it to the hospital, and the nurses let her stand in the room as his lips puckered and his chest caved in. Told me she cradled him in her arms, and that he reached up and stroked her face just a second before the heart monitor cracked into a thin line.

After that, she just broke apart. She ran away from the foster home, hopped trains all around the city, and fell in with a group of other homeless teenagers. Drugs, fights, long nights spent shivering in the cold. St. Therese wasn't her first state-appointed home. She did four months at Sunset Gardens, an inpatient mental hospital for teenagers. They figured out that she'd tried to kill herself a few times and locked her up.

That got me. The suicide.

She's attempted it. I've only thought about it.

When I asked her how she dealt with everything, she took off her shirt, exposing her breasts, and showed me the scars that dot her skin like birthmarks. Welts and cuts and snaky patterns all over her arms and stomach. And a big one, an X, right over her heart.

It was the cutting that finally did her in.

My stomach clenched. I tried to picture her, knife in hand, running the blade along her flesh as blood pooled out. I'd seen scarification before. It was nothing new. But seeing it on Clare made me feel sick. Her chubby face and body, her bright eyes. Still can't believe it. From my place on the bed, I stared at her wrists and for the first time noticed the skinny lines shooting across her veins like train tracks. Can't get them outta my head.

"Don't look so scared," she said to me. "I'm not gonna kill myself anytime soon, so just chill."

Came back into my room and tried to do a little of my history report. Sister Ellen called a group meeting again, so now I have to sit through that. I don't mind listening and talking like we do on these nights, but when we're all together—me and Bram and Marty and Clare—I start wondering why we're so unlucky. I mean, what did we do to deserve all this shit? Why are we "inner city" and not "safe suburbs"?

1/22

ESCAPE

this is the place
I saw it in a dream
a big white house
surrounded by green
trees up high
a clear bright sky
a place to watch
the bluebirds fly—
kids like me
we ain't taught to
hope
we just spend our days
learning how to
cope
but ask me to tell you
what I see
when darkness reaches out
for me
it's not this searing
mediocrity
or what other people
expect it to be—

it's a yard
a dog
a home that's mine
a kitchen table
and a bottle of wine
a closet filled with
clothes that fit
a little fireplace
warm and lit
I picture myself
lying on the grass
watching clouds and
sunshine pass
I'll think of the city
far and away
all cramped and humid
and steely gray
but I'll save the memory
for another day

this is the place
a country of my own
where hate is outlawed
and sadness rides alone
where black and white and
the in-between
hear the Voice
and not the scream
where guns and knives

don't exist
and danger vanishes
like morning mist
where kids are fed and
families stay
and all the lost
find their way
where fear and pain
are both rejected
and unity is
resurrected

this is the place
one day I'll escape
and I'll know a world
without heartbreak

1/24

IT HAPPENED AGAIN. Tonight there was another shoot-out in the neighborhood, this one a block away, at the housing project. We were eating dinner in the kitchen when we heard the shots—three flat cracks. I jumped up. Bram and Marty got still. And Clare just about spit up her food.

"Not again," Sister Ellen said.

We all got silent. Didn't move a muscle. Shouts and screams started piercing the air outside. They filtered through the living room from the window that looks out onto the street. Sounded like a man was crying for his life.

"Jesus," Bram said.

And then another shot exploded, along with a clatter of glass.

A bullet slammed through the living room window.

"Get down!" Sister Ellen screamed. "Now! Move!"

Me and Bram knew what to do. We threw ourselves flat onto the floor, covering our heads with our hands. Marty and Clare panicked a little and fumbled as they tried to fit under the table. A third round boomed, followed by the screech of tires. Then it was over.

Sister Ellen was on the phone with the police when Bram looked up at me. We both knew it had been a close one.

A few minutes later I slipped into the living room and looked around. My heart was beating fast. I saw the white drapes all torn and messy, charred at one end with black. They billowed away from the single, wide hole sucking cold air into the house. The window glass was shattered like a spiderweb.

Sister Ellen screamed for me from the kitchen, telling me to get back. When I turned, I saw her standing on the threshold, totally spooked. She wouldn't step foot in the living room.

I told her to relax because I knew what I was doing. I tiptoed to the front door and put my hand on the knob. Bram ran past Sister Ellen and came right to my side. We looked at each other, both of us fearing what we would see if we opened the door. But what if somebody needed help? What if one of the kids from the building across the way had gotten hit? I turned the knob. And that's when I saw the blood. A little puddle of it, smeared right across the curb. The body was out of eyeshot, but the victim's hand was resting against the ground, palm up and fingers splayed. A man's hand. I didn't wanna see the rest of him.

I'm up in my room now. Keep looking out the

window. Lights are painting the sky red. Crime scene people are in the living room looking for the bullet. They think it's lodged in the wall. It was probably from a .38, and those bullets suck.

Sister Ellen told us that tomorrow afternoon cops from one of the downtown precincts are coming here to talk to us. I guess it's necessary. For now, we're all under lockdown and can't leave the building. Not the way I wanted to spend my Wednesday night.

1/25

OH GOD. JESUS. Please help me.

Someone, help me.

I don't know what to do. Don't know what to say or write or think.

Losing my mind. Feel like dying. Or killing.

Marty and Clare are knocking on my door right now, trying to get my attention, trying to stop me from doing something crazy. But there's no help now. No one who can save me. Sitting here at my desk in the near-dark, writing blindly. I'm seeing red. My hands are trembling so much.

How could this happen? Why?

We were in the living room downstairs, waiting for the cops to show up, the ones who were supposed to give a talk about safety in the neighborhood. I was already feeling queasy. Afraid one of them might come in here and recognize me from all those interviews I did on TV and in the newspapers. My mind was gone. Then the doorbell rang. The cops came in and I heard Sister Ellen talking with them in the hallway. Mumbled words. A welcoming. I tried not to pay attention.

And then it happened.

Sister Ellen came into the living room, trailed by

three uniformed cops. I stared each of them in the eyes. It took only a moment for my heart to stop beating. I gasped, thinking I was seeing things again. But no—this was *fucking real.*

One of the cops was Mickey Pesaturo.

The man who killed my brother. The man who lifted his gun to Julio's chest and fired. The man who—

Oh God. What's happening to me?

Can't concentrate with them banging on my bedroom door like that. Go away. Get the fuck outta here. Leave me alone. Please.

Mickey Pesaturo. I've written his name so many times, spoken it out loud, but never did I think I'd come face to face with him again.

He stood there, glancing around. So close to me. I could've reached out and touched him.

Strangled him.

Stabbed him.

He looked at me, and there was a quick flash in his eyes. Shock.

We stared at each other.

And then I took a step forward. The world around me disappeared. The walls became houses, the ground became concrete. I was standing there again, on that street corner in the Bronx. "You," I whispered. "You . . ."

He swallowed hard. The brown hair, the blue eyes, the thin face. *Him.*

My breath came in short harsh gasps, tearing

through me, making me tremble. I forgot every-thing. Didn't even remember myself. One voice in my mind was shouting for revenge, for vengeance. Another was wailing. Staring at him. Shaking my head. I didn't want to cry but the tears poured down.

I crumbled.

"You son of a bitch," I whispered. And then, louder: "You're a fucking killer! A murderer!"

From behind, Bram was telling me to chill. He reached for my shoulders, tried to hold me down.

Mickey Pesaturo didn't know what to do. You'd think he'd have wanted to turn around and run. In-stead he just stood there, staring back at me. His eyes never left my face.

And then Mickey Pesaturo spoke. He removed his cap and took a step toward me. Said my name as if he wanted something: "Luz?"

Sister Ellen was telling me to calm down. Her hands were on my shoulders too.

Mickey Pesaturo said it again. "Luz."

But I was shrieking. Called him a fucker, a son of a bitch. And before I could stop myself, I charged into him, ripping from Bram's grasp and hurling myself forward. My fists shot out. I grazed his shoul-der with all my strength and then went for his eyes. I wanted to do it right then and there. Wanted his blood pooling over my hands. But Sister Ellen stopped me. She jumped between us, held my arms.

Bram and Marty and Clare came around to calm me down.

Can't even write what I felt. A trance. A black tunnel. A physical sickness. Thought I might die right there at Mickey Pesaturo's feet like Julio did.

Don't know if he said anything else. It was madness. Tears clouding my vision. Heart drilling through my ribs. I glanced around at the shocked faces and realized that I had lost control. Become a monster, the girl I used to be, full of rage and danger.

Ran out of there, flew up the stairs. Locked myself in my room.

They're still outside, all of them pleading with me to speak. I can hear Clare's voice right now. Can't face them. Don't think I'll ever be able to again. God—what is this? It's been an hour but the emotions are still ripping me apart. Not sure what I'll do if I step beyond my door. Seeing knives and blood and hearing gunshots ricochet in the darkness. It's a madness I can't handle. I'm on fire.

I'm burning up. . . .

1/31? 2/1?
(WHO GIVES A SHIT?)

WELCOME TO MY WORLD. . . .

full moon rises in the midnight sky
and on the streets
sirens start to cry
starin' out my window at the cold concrete
but deep inside my mind
I'm feelin' all the heat
memories play
and demons stay
and before I know it
I've got another beast to slay
can't explain it in simple terms
'cause when I think about reality
my anger burns
I could tell you about my life
this sweet private hell
but wait a minute
I've got a story to tell
Mama's in the kitchen tryin'
to figure out the bills
one dollar to the next is a test of wills
baby's cryin' and losing more weight
but he can't eat if there's

no food on his plate
the money in my pocket won't
feed this family
but take it, Mom,
you need it more than me
don't ask questions and
wipe away that tear
my old man?
he ain't ever been here
saw him once but
the memory is bad
he left me bleedin'
hey fuck you, Dad!

walk out the door and
step outside
prepare myself for another wild ride
darkness is colored by
red and blue light
two cruisers at the corner
and the cops are white
they look me in the eye
as I walk by
they see danger but
I don't know why
maybe it's my clothes or
the dreads in my hair
the chain around my neck
or the skin that I wear

I'd try to say somethin'
if I could
but no one has a voice
in this forgotten neighborhood
here's the truth: the women are scared
their husbands beat them
but the system don't care
they have their kids and
build up resistance
but life don't cut it
on public assistance
the mothers get younger and
they don't feel
the fathers get desperate so
they start to deal
powders, pills, blunts and smack
the cash keeps comin' and
there's no way back
young men believin' that
this life is a drag
they get in too deep and
leave the streets in a bag
down at the corner
hidden in the dark
I see the girls who used to
play in the park
they all grown up now
and ready to bail
but it's gotta hurt

when your lips are for sale
they go down easy
and come up wet
it's all pimps and pain
and shit they'll never forget
on to the shelter where
the homeless run
salvation's missing and
the souls are numb
there's a guy outside
with tracks on his arm
ninety degrees but he's
tryin' to stay warm
his days are numbered
he's beatin' the clock
and he takes out a pipe and
puts a sizzle to the rock

I pass the church but I
don't think about grace
'cause God won't visit
this hellish place
old ladies with their Bibles
kneel and pray
they need false hope to
survive another day
ain't no time to be
saved
when the world's on fire

look at these streets
where's your Messiah?
white out the blood with
a hand to the cross
but don't ever forget that
survival's the Boss
it ain't about heaven or
the Virgin Mary
a virgin? here?
that shit is scary
okay enough said
enough done
no more preachin'
so pardon the pun
I just think it's wrong that
we live like this
one breath away
from death's dark kiss
so where do I go?
what do I do?
why do I even bother
askin' you?
unless you live here
you ain't got a clue
cops come around but
when they do
it's madness
chaos
a white man's zoo

they look at us and see
indecency
I look at them and see
the enemy
I could stand out here and
wait for rain
let it wash away
some of my pain
but there ain't no time now
I've gotta bounce
can you hear it in the distance?
shots rang out. . . .

11:41 P.M.
Any questions?

2/3

NINE DAYS AGO, I saw the man who killed you. And I think he killed me too.

2/14

HIS FACE IS still there, in front of me. I see it whenever I close my eyes. I see it in my dreams and when I look up at the sky. Even as I'm flipping through the pages of my notebook in homeroom. He's there, waiting.

Mickey Pesaturo.

Stood so close to me. Spoke my name. Saw the rage in me.

Weeks gone by, and I still can't get over it. Like I'm in a tunnel with no light and no air. No release. I can't see anything except that one scene—the cops walking through the door and our eyes meeting. It's taken me this long to accept that it even happened and that Mickey Pesaturo watched me fall apart. Most of all, that's what bothers me. I hate that I let myself lose control because now everybody knows the truth—that I don't have it all together, that I'm dangerous and still fucked up. I don't wanna admit it, but it's totally true.

I'm thinking a lot about the past, about the girl I used to be before I came to St. Therese. All the violence. The fighting. Like nothing in the world mattered so long as I got my way. I thought I'd gotten beyond that. Buried it. But the rage I felt the other night, standing so close to Mickey Pesaturo, made me realize that there's no escape from it.

Truth is, I don't wanna be that girl anymore. Worked too hard to put her away and become someone else. But everything is coming back to me, a flood, and I can't hold those waters back. Anything might set me off. Yesterday, in math class, the sub kept telling me to pay attention because I was just staring out the window, thinking. I got all angry inside. Felt like I was gonna stand up and hurl a desk at her, pound her face in with my fists. I didn't, but I was that close.

Tick me off and I'll fuck you up. My new secret motto. I'm not proud of it.

It's been like that here at home too. Bram keeps his distance. Marty stares at me. Clare just smiles and kinda waits for me to speak. Sister Ellen is a whole different story, because she's been trying to get me to talk to her, to open up, which I just can't seem to do. I'm afraid I might scare her if I tell her what's going on in my head. God knows I've been scaring myself.

I already know the facts. If I let myself lose control, if I bust into a fight with someone or start acting up, I can get transferred outta here into juvenile detention. I'll be eighteen in like four months, so how stupid would that be? Thing is, the mind plays tricks. I'm learning that now. I see Mickey Pesaturo's face everywhere, and it makes me so damn angry.

He's out there, living his life and not feeling a thing. And I'm here, cracking my skull and trying to keep it all together. Am I just supposed to be cool with that?

No. Impossible. And too dangerous. I have to find a way out of this, 'cause if I don't, I'll end up hurting someone. Maybe even myself.

P.S. Happy Valentine's Day.

10:18 P.M.

Burning up. Letting the fire cut through me. There's a reason I'm so scared of it. When it happens, I go too far. . . .

A memory.

No, wait. A confession. Consider this my first one:

Midnight. A chill wind. There was no moon over Manhattan. I was sitting in the passenger seat of the beat-up Toyota, listening to my girls hash out the details of the plan. My fingers were numb. I kept flexing them because I knew the knife would feel heavy in my hands. I was with my crew. My family. That meant anything could happen. And everything always did.

Jesse was in the driver's seat. She had pulled the car into a spot and cut the headlights. "It's that one, right over there," she said, and pointed. "The target."

I glanced out my side window. The little deli was at First Avenue and Eleventh Street, open twenty-four hours. We'd driven down from the Bronx. People didn't know us here and that meant a clean getaway.

Marisol was sitting in the backseat, drinking a forty. Her dark hair was cut short. There were pockmarks on her face from acne. Sitting beside her was Lydia. You look at her, tall and lean, and see something puny, like a frail bird. In truth, she was cold and knew how to handle every corner of the street. She didn't say anything. She was loading a cartridge into the .38 she had stolen from one of her ex-boyfriends.

"When they see the gun, they'll know exactly what you want," Jesse said. "Just jump the counter, grab the cash and split. I'll be waiting here." She always involved me in these late-night "outings." I was the most fearless one of all. I had already lost almost everything, so losing some more wouldn't matter. I could look anybody in the eye, ignore the tears, and do what needed to be done. This was business. This was survival. Luz Cordero felt nothing and she never looked back.

Outside, me and Marisol and Lydia crossed the street to the deli. From a short distance, I peered in through the glass door and saw a skinny Chinese lady leaning over the register. She'd be easy to pull down. I lit a cigarette, took a few fast drags, then turned to face my girls. Marisol pulled a ski mask over her face and ran into the deli. Watching from outside, I saw her spray the little surveillance camera with shaving cream. And then me and Lydia moved in. We threw open the door so hard the glass panes shattered.

"Hands up!" Lydia roared, pulling the gun from her jacket.

The Chinese woman must've been forty, but in that moment, she aged about ten years. She threw her arms toward the ceiling. Her jaw dropped. She was trembling like a leaf. "Please, no hurt, no hurt," she kept saying.

A man came out of a back room. He was about to turn back, but Lydia leveled the gun directly at him. "You move, I blow you away. Understand?"

The man nodded and moved to the woman's side. "Understand," he said quietly.

I jumped the counter and pushed them both aside. With one hard kick, the cash register sprang open, and I started hauling bundles of cash into my pockets, moving quickly, never glancing up.

"Hurry," Marisol said. She was standing by the door, keeping guard.

Suddenly the woman's sobs turned into angry grunts. She screamed at me to stop. Called me a bitch. Then she took a step toward me and lashed out at my hair with her hands. I didn't feel it. I didn't even have time to care. But Lydia wasn't in the mood for drama. In one motion, she leaned across the counter and punched the woman. She waved the gun in their faces, saying, "You want this in your head? Huh? Huh?"

The woman gave a little scream. She stumbled back, into the man's arms. Blood dribbled from her nose.

Marisol gave me the hand signal indicating that a full thirty seconds had passed. I hopped out from behind the counter. We started outside.

The couple was huddled in the corner. Lydia, playing it cool, reached out and lifted a carton of cigarettes into her jacket. She never took her eyes off the man. He just stared. His arms circled the woman's body. He and Lydia seemed to be conversing wordlessly, each aware of the other's thoughts. And then he uttered a single word: "Spic."

"What was that?" she said.

He spat on the floor. "Dirty spic!"

Lydia raised the gun again. She took three steps forward. . . .

I waited, thinking she would open fire, thinking blood was going to flow over the walls in bright red spurts. I urged her to forget it and come on. But her eyes hardened and she said, "Someone needs to teach these Chinks a lesson."

They were cowering together, the man and the woman. Lydia moved her arm a little, just out of their path, and shot out the telephone mounted on the wall. A deafening crack. There was an explosion of plastic and screws and a flying white cord.

I never faltered. Didn't even jump. Did I laugh, seeing how the Chinese man doubled over, clutching his chest in fear? Maybe. But fuck it–they meant nothing to me.

The three of us ran out of the deli and into the waiting car. Jesse revved the engine. We went speeding up First Avenue, screaming and sharing high fives, throwing our handkerchiefs to the wind. I grabbed handfuls of cash from my pockets. I held them up like a hundred prizes.

"How much?" Marisol said. "Count it! Come on!"

So I sat there, counting. In all, $1,487–a literal fortune to us.

By the time we hit the highway five minutes later, I had forgotten our victims. Hell, I didn't care about my own life–why would I care about theirs? It felt good letting the rage burn from my veins. It felt good knowing someone was hurting as much as me. Nothing else mattered.

In the distance, sirens wailed. . . .

11:55 P.M.

I can still hear them, wailing louder than ever.

2/16

THEY KEEP ASKING me to talk about it. Marty, Bram, Clare. Sister Ellen. I even got a phone call from Anne Burns today. When are they gonna understand that there's nothing to talk about? I'm too embarrassed about the way I acted. Too angry to think back on the whole experience.

Just leave me alone, people. Let me burn.

2/19

IT TURNS OUT Clare's the one with guts. Go figure. She was waiting for me outside school this morning, and when we spotted each other she said, "So what the hell is up with you?" I told her I didn't wanna talk about it. She made a sour face. Rolled her eyes. It was seven-thirty, and we both had twenty minutes to kill before first period. I didn't have the heart to turn away from her and leave because I know she really cares. Marty and Bram do too, but it's a different thing with girls. She admitted that she'd been asking Sister Ellen about me, and Sister Ellen told her to just give me time and space. Clare said that's the problem—too much space and people start to get lost.

Between cigarettes and sips from her water bottle, I opened up a little bit. More than I expected to. I told her I'm worried about the feelings I've been having, the restless rage. I don't think she knew about some of the things I did before coming to St. Therese, like holding up the deli downtown, but she didn't act surprised. She said she could totally relate to me and that sometimes she feels like she's gonna explode too. That's when she has to stop herself from cutting at the skin along her arms or going out and finding someone who'll sell her ecstasy for real cheap so she can get high and forget everything. It happens when she thinks about the past.

But instead of dwelling on it like me, Clare bleeds it out. She does whatever she has to in order to overcome it. Sometimes she draws. Sometimes she writes. She told me that last month she got all violent inside, but instead of reaching for a knife she went down to the chapel and just stared at the statues for a long time and prayed. Point is, she gets it out of her system before she can hurt herself.

I understand where she's coming from, but I'm not like that. I can't make myself forget Mickey Pesaturo or Julio and the gunshot that took his life. It's like a maze. One thought leads into another, and then come the memories. And before I know it I'm lost and angry and feeling the way I do now.

We ended up cutting first period and hanging out in the third-floor girls' bathroom. It's the warmest, and security guards usually don't do their random checks until midmorning. Sitting there on the floor behind the stalls, I shared my thoughts. Clare stayed silent most of the time, letting me talk. For a while it got quiet between us and I had to hide my face in my hands. Thought I was gonna cry. Can't understand it, but the sad feeling just came and sank into my bones. I didn't shed any tears, though. Held it all in, like usual.

But then I did something weird.

I asked Clare if I could see her scars again, asked her if I could touch the little welts and patches of cut skin.

The question just came out. The chaos inside me broke up, like I needed to lose myself in someone else's pain for once. She dropped her shirt off her shoulders and showed me the scar above her heart. It was the same purplish color as before, a jagged X. Pressed my finger to it, imagined the blade sinking in and cutting away all the confusion. For the first time, it didn't gross me out. And if I winced at all, it was because I understood the need to go that far.

2/21

COULDN'T STAND IT in school today, so I cut out before fifth period and took the train all the way uptown. At first I told myself I didn't know where I was going, but I guess I knew all along. There's this little shop on Third Avenue and Ninety-eighth Street I used to go to when I was living in the Bronx. Me and some of the other girls in the crew. It's right next to a bodega, down a flight of stairs and through a narrow alleyway. Most people don't even know it exists. Probably used to be a basement. Now it's stocked with army knives, box cutters and guns. Buy anything you want for the right price. The owner, an old Spanish guy with a patch over his eye, didn't recognize me, thank God. Felt weird being there. Edgy. A little nervous. But I had to do it. Couldn't stop myself. I had five bucks in my pocket and just enough change to get home.

I bought a switchblade.

2/22

THE SHARP EDGE. The little click it makes
when I press it against my wrists. Holding the blade
in my hands reminds me . . .

That cold December night, frost on the window
and snow falling outside. We were in our apartment
above the deli, and there was no heat again. The living room stank. Beer bottles littered the floor near
the couch, where Mom was passed out from too
much booze. I knew something was wrong. I saw it
in your attitude, the way you moved around so tense
and angry. Your mind was crowded. Lying there on
your bed watching TV, I glimpsed you pacing the
floor and nervously biting your nails.

"What's wrong?" I asked.

"Nothing," you snapped. "I'm fine."

I called your name. You just shook your head.
You wanted to be left alone but you didn't wanna be
lonely. I was fourteen and felt the same way.

Outside on the street, a garbage truck was col-
lecting last week's trash.

Finally you said, "I'm in trouble, Luz."

"What?" I sat up, scared.

And then you told me what I didn't wanna hear.
There was a fight happening down at the park, a

scheduled battle between the guys in our neighbor-hood and one of the other gangs. No good reason for it. Just words passed between enemies, teenage thugs who had too much time on their hands. That was how all the fights started. And why all the shots rang out in the dark.

You weren't a member of the crew yet. You hung out with the tough players and wanted in, but at six-teen you still had to prove yourself. No father to teach you about life, you became a man on your own and learned the lessons before anyone could tell you to slow down.

I said, "Please don't go." Whispering it quietly at first, then begging you to stay inside even as you ranted on about the point of it all. It had nothing to do with proving yourself, you said. It was about throwing out the fear and building up resistance. You saw our lives in the inner city as doomed, hope-less. You said no one could escape without fighting. It wasn't only the other neighborhood guys who posed a threat. It was the cops too. The system. De-signed to keep us down. Those were your words.

I watched as you reached into your dresser drawer and took out the switchblade. You had tried to buy a gun but didn't have enough money. The blade would have to do. Standing there, you flicked it once, staring at the thin steel edge. You were re-membering your old friends—Lonnie and Raymond—who had died the year before in a similar gang battle.

Both of them stabbed in the neck, their throats slit. Took three days for their mothers to wash the blood off the pavement.

You turned and stared at me. You saw the anxiety in my eyes, the fear of losing you. And you said, "I have to do this."

What scared me most was the look in your eyes, the crazed desperation to let it all out. Filled with pent-up rage, you were searching for release. It was a need, a hunger. If you didn't let it burn up in a fight, something worse might happen.

I never thought the feeling would be contagious.

You came up to me, gave me a quick hug. Said, "Be good, okay?" like it was the last time. And then you were gone.

I lay there in the dark, filling the shadows with prayers. When I heard the sirens echoing in the distance, I cried against my pillow and let the sobs wrack my chest. I pictured the switchblade in your hands. Pictured it falling from your fingers in a rush of bodies and too much weight. Would you remember to cover your face, shield your jugular from someone else's rage?

Two hours passed. Then I heard the door open and close, your footsteps echoing on the floor. You came into the bedroom breathing hard. Even in the dark, I smelled the sweat dripping off your clothes and sensed the violence of it all. I was too afraid to move. You were too battered to speak. You undressed

73

and lowered yourself onto the floor beside the bed. Cold, I reached down and put my hand on your arm. And then I felt it: a little line of blood dripping from one of your wounds. It flowed and swirled, sticky against my fingers. When dawn broke over the sky, I was still awake. And in the first light of morning, I saw the switchblade on top of your dresser, stained and caked with red, sitting beside a framed picture of us.

2/23

DON'T SPEAK

listen chill
keep your mind still
judge me later and
think what you will
this is my heart
I've pulled the last stitch
I've kept my lips sealed
but now it's time to bitch
they expect it to vanish
my deep dark past
but the memories stay
from the first to the last
picture the dawn
all cold and blue
when I close my eyes
it reminds me of you
my heart, my brother
too far away to touch
just one more day
is that asking too much?
I'm shattered like glass
every last edgy shard

picking up the pieces
is getting too hard
why was I dealt
this ugly card?

watch what you say
get to class
do your work
it's fail or pass
every rule is like
a kick in the ass
what do they want?
what do they mean?
I'm feeling too old
at seventeen
so yeah—I know
it could be a lot worse
that's what they say
but I'm driving this hearse
the road is dark
ain't no way to switch lanes
I can't stop or speed
'cause these aren't my games
it happens like this
when I think too deep
so just hush
leave me
and please don't speak

2/26

THERE'S BLOOD ON my hands.

Lines of it under my nails. A bright streak on my palm. I can still see it oozing from the wound.

I didn't want it to happen. Even now, sitting at the kitchen table with this damn ice pack on my forehead, I can swear that none of it was my fault.

I was coming out of sixth period this afternoon when I heard the commotion. The fourth-floor hallway, just outside the cafeteria. All of a sudden, people started rushing past the staircase and voices were going up. Another pointless fight. That's what I thought until I rounded the corner and saw Marty being slammed up against a locker.

Corey Nolan and Jeff Serica, both seniors and asshole bullies, had Marty pinned back. They've called him names in the past, screaming out "faggot" and "queen" whenever he walked by. He just doesn't know how to defend himself. When I first saw him against the locker this afternoon, there was blood dripping from his nose and a cut on his cheek. He was crying. So much fear in his eyes.

That's when everything around me froze. Total standstill. I got a sick feeling in my stomach, like I wanted to cry and scream at the same time. For a second I couldn't move. Just watched as Jeff threw Marty an uppercut to the jaw and Corey tried kicking him in the nuts. Students gathered around, some of them yelling in fear but most of them egging the fight on. Then Corey put his hands around Marty's throat and threw him to the floor. Called him a faggot. They started kicking him too, and I saw Marty trying to cover his face with his hands, like a helpless little kid on a playground.

My rage boiled over. Started shaking. Felt my heart pounding. I dropped my backpack and the books I'd been holding and ran down the hall. Thick with bodies but I pushed everyone outta my way. It was like a riot in slow motion. A part of me knew better, but there was nothing to do at that point. No stopping me.

I tackled Corey first. Slammed into him from behind and we both went flying against the locker. I jabbed him in the eyes with my fingers. He shook his head, stunned. Then I kneed him in the crotch. I felt Jeff's hands on my shoulders, pulling me back. I turned and his fist bounced off the side of my head. I cut him with a blow to the stomach.

In the middle of all the screaming, I heard someone yell out my name. It was Bram. He was standing in the crowd, telling me to stop. I couldn't. Everything was racing through me. Then the switchblade tumbled out of my pocket and onto the floor. I bent down and picked it up. Flicked it once. Lashed out at Jeff and sliced him across his forehead.

Blood. Lots of it.

"Come on!" I kept saying as he cupped the wound with his hands. "You want some more? Come on!"

He jumped back and I was screaming at him, hoping he would strike again. He didn't. I waved the switchblade like a trophy, forgetting everyone and everything around me. My heart, beating so fast. Sweat in my eyes. I felt the heat rush through my skin, blazing and intense. It was the fire, sparked the day I saw Mickey Pesaturo.

Marty was still on the floor, and by the time I got to him, the security guards were at my side, grabbing my hands and pulling me back. Every eye was on me.

Sat in the principal's office and waited for nothing. They sent me home. Suspended for two days. Marty was taken to the hospital, where he got a few stitches and some pills for the pain.

I had to explain my side of it to Sister Ellen. Not much to say. She told me we'd talk about it tomorrow, after I'd cooled down. I'm not allowed to leave the house unless it explodes.

Quiet now. Almost six o'clock. Anne Burns called an hour ago and said that even though I acted in what she believes was sort of self-defense, the fight's gonna go down on my probation record. Marty told her that I saved his life today, and Bram and Clare stood up for me too. The security guards at school confiscated my switchblade and I won't be getting it back. So, for now, I'm safe.

Wish I felt better about the whole thing. I'm not sorry for kicking Jeff's ass and kneeing Corey in the nuts, but I still feel guilty because I fucked up and let people down. Sister Ellen. Anne Burns. And mostly myself.

Staring at my dinner plate as I write this. Can't eat. My stomach's tense and my hands are sore. Looking forward to going to bed tonight. With any luck, I won't wake up.

8:00 P.M.

Oh shit! Ten minutes ago Marty asked everyone to come into the living room—me, Bram, Clare and Sister Ellen. We all sat down. He stood in front of us, all bruised up, and just busted out with the words. "I'm bisexual," he said. "Anybody got a problem with that?" Clare shrugged—no big deal. I cracked a smile. Then we all looked at Bram, who was moving around in his chair, looking uncomfortable. After a minute he shook his head and said, "No, man. You be who you gotta be."

Marty was cool about the whole thing. Told us he's tired of hiding it, and that's why he got jumped today. He was passing out flyers for the new GLBTU club that he's starting in school. Jeff and Corey saw him, warned him to stop, and when Marty didn't, they threw down a beating.

Sister Ellen shocked me the most. She held Marty's hands and told him that she understood. She said that we're his family—and families like ours stick together. No preaching, no religious stuff. Then she took him into her office and closed the door. They're still in there, talking.

I'll be the next one to sit in that therapy chair.

2/27

Got called down to a Twisted Sister session this morning just like I predicted. That's when Sister Ellen does one-on-one counseling, and we've all been through it. She hasn't called me in for one of these chats since I first got here. Today's talk was the toughest we'd ever had. She didn't dance around the issues that usually make me uncomfortable. Started out by telling me that I've spent the past month in a depressed state, and that I haven't been the same since seeing Mickey Pesaturo. Normal, she said, but it's time to get over it and move on.

Her words. Exactly.

She understands about the fight. I defended Marty. I saw injustice and tried to right it. But she thinks I could've handled it better and not drawn blood. When she asked me where I got the switchblade, I confessed. Told her I couldn't help myself. She nodded slowly and said, "So did you get it all out of your system? Did cutting up those two guys at school make you feel better?"

Not really. Or maybe a little. Not because I wanted to do it, but because I had to.

She said, "You didn't have to. You chose to do it.

82

You've been wanting to beat somebody up for the last month. And you knew you would, eventually. That's why you bought the blade."

I told her I didn't know why I bought the blade. Certain things–feelings–you just can't explain. It made me feel safer, stronger. Fighting is the only thing I know how to do. That's how I survived most of my life. And seeing Mickey Pesaturo again triggered that response in me.

And then she read my mind and told me that no matter what I think, I'm not the crazy girl who protested her way through the streets anymore. That part of me is gone. She said I crashed yesterday because I haven't been honest with myself about a lot of things. That's when the conversation turned to Julio and the night he died. I didn't talk about it, though. Still can't bring myself to do that. She asked me why, and I told her it's complicated.

She said, "You loved him, I understand that. He was really the only family you had. He understood the same things you did–the injustices and the hardships of being a kid from the inner city. But there were also things about Julio that you didn't like, Luz. And those things explain a lot."

I felt my face get hot and red. Asked her if I could leave, and she said no. Her words threw me off, scared me. We sat there in the silence. One minute . . . two. Finally she asked me if I understood what she meant, and I nodded.

That was the main point of today's session—I have to learn to tell myself the truth. But it's not as easy as it sounds.

Stuck here in my room, waiting for the hours to slip by. It's only three-thirty. I'm basically under house arrest till tomorrow night. Can't even set foot on the front stoop. Like I'm in solitary fucking confinement at Rikers.

Here's the first lesson: loneliness sucks.

7:25 P.M.

The little chapel is attached to the house. You have to go through Sister Ellen's first-floor bedroom and across a narrow hallway to reach it. There's an altar and three rows of chairs. A few statues. Crucifix up high. Sitting here is like leaving the neighborhood, even if only for a few minutes. Forget the inner city and think of the inner soul—that's what Bram says. Was his idea that I chill with the saints for a while.

I haven't thought about God in a long time. I know that sounds strange living in a place like this, with a nun, but even prayers remind me of Julio and my mother. They were both always whispering to some angel or saint, asking for help even when they knew it wasn't coming. Even when they knew they were beyond help.

But that's not why I came to the chapel tonight.

Despite everything that's happened, there's a part of me that believes I'll make it through. All along I've believed that. The thing is, there're certain steps I have to take to get that hidden part of myself out into the open, and the whole idea of it scares me.

Truth. Honesty. If that's what it's about, I guess I have to start right now.

Thinking back on yesterday, on the fight, makes me feel guilty. The rage is just an excuse for keeping my own secrets buried. Even if it hadn't been for Marty's sake, I probably would've ended up bashing in someone's face just to get the bad emotions out of my blood. When you're in pain, you play your own game. It's a creed on the streets. It's the reason any teenager starts a brawl in school, gets hurt and suspended. Or expelled. No mystery to it. We all know why we do the things we do.

Julio, can you hear me? I'm thinking about so many things. What would you say to me right now? You proud that I fought off those two guys? Probably. I learned more about fighting from you than I did from being in the gang. When I look over these pages, it seems like you only did good things. It's true you did a lot of good things, but there's a lot about you that I've chosen to forget. And it's not fair to me. Little by little, I'm starting to understand that. Yesterday, the fighting and the rage—it's not who I wanna be. It's who I think I *have* to be to survive. But where has it gotten me? Where did it get you?

I miss you more than I can say. You know that. And sitting here in this chapel, listening to the silence and coming to terms with everything . . . I think maybe I've said my first prayer in a long time.

2/28

Woke up early but didn't leave my room. Instead, I went through some of my old boxes, the things I took from home right after I was sent to live here. And for the first time in more than seven months, I looked at a picture of Julio. Dozens of pictures. His face. His eyes. His scars.

Remembering is painful. But not remembering hurts even more. When I stare at the pictures of him now, this is what flashes through my mind:

A secret meeting. An initiation of the most painful kind. Agony was the test, blood the reward.

We had gathered in droves at the entrance to Pelham Bay Park—me, Marisol, Jesse, Lydia, Deena, Angela and a bunch of other girls from the neighborhood. All of us about sixteen. The boys were already waiting there: Stevie, Nick, Jesus, Juan, Cheney, Billy, Fred. And Julio.

Julio, seventeen years old, with a buzzed head and fear in his eyes. A gang initiate. But really a kid with anger in his heart and bad plans on his mind.

Beer cans littered the tall blades of grass, and there was the scent of cigarettes and pot in the air. The boys looked excited. Stevie, the oldest member

87

of his gang, stepped into the circle behind the parking lot and brought the ceremony to a start. He ushered Julio forward. They bunted fists and embraced each other silently. Words were exchanged. Then Stevie stepped away and lit a cigarette.

Julio scanned the waiting faces. His gaze stopped on mine. He didn't speak, but I knew—I know it even now, years later—that he was asking me to forgive him. He was telling me that it was too late, that he could find no other way out of the hopeless maze into which we'd been born. And so this day marked the beginning of his new life. A life that would pull him further away from me and closer to the statistics of the streets.

I turned and looked at Marisol. She pushed herself against me as the other girls drew nearer. "Don't worry," one of them said. "Julio knows what he's doing." And I believed it. I believed that maybe he'd become a gang member and avoid the dangers. That he'd fight the battles without getting caught or hurt. "Yeah," I whispered. "He'll be okay."

It happened quickly.

Stevie shouted a word, a command, and the boys shot forward like animals. They grunted. They spat. They kicked dirt up from the ground. Julio disappeared beneath a cloak of fists and legs, his body a punching bag, his knees buckling beneath him. It sounded like stones were hitting a wall. He tried to scream but his words were muffled by the violence.

A crack. An uppercut. A guttural choke. Like being put through a paper shredder slowly, Marisol said.

I watched it happen, backing away and then forcing myself to stand still. The sun peeked over the darkness, a single ray of gold. Through it I could see drops of blood falling from within the tangled mass of bodies. Julio's head surfaced once. Three fists powered it back down into the beating. He tried moving his arms up to shield his face, but their weight was too much for him. He cried out. He screeched. But he didn't beg for it to stop because doing so would disqualify him from the fold.

So many fists. So much rage.

"Oh man," Marisol said. "That's heavy shit. Look at how he's taking it!"

The other kids cheered Julio on. They pointed at the blood and his torn patches of clothing and saw a hero. But in that moment, I forgot the symbolism of it all and saw the sacrifice. The fists didn't represent the strength of the inner city. Julio, kicked and humiliated, wasn't a metaphor for battle. That was the gang mentality, though. It was their language, their own savage poetry. That was how they formed friendships and made families. And if he'd had his own family, I thought, maybe Julio wouldn't have felt the need to find another one.

Maybe I wouldn't have felt the need either.

Two minutes later, it was over. The boys walked away from the circle one by one, shaking out their hands and cheering the successful initiation. Julio was on the ground, panting like a dog, on all fours. Blood—everywhere. It dripped from his nose and swirled in a crimson line down the side of his head. His shirt was ripped almost completely off his body. He stood up, stumbled and closed his eyes. It was all about the body. The brain didn't matter—who needed to think in our neighborhood? To survive, you had to know how to run and fight and fuck someone up. That day, a man was made in the inner city.

Stevie ran up to him, patted his shoulders. "You done good, Cordero." He held up Julio's arm and roused the crowd. The other boys gathered around him and threw up high fives. Admirable, they said. Impressive. Julio had taken the beating and survived. Now he knew he could face any fear or obstacle. He could face the streets and challenge them.

I watched as Stevie reached into his jacket and pulled out a gun. A small Glock, its silver handle gleaming in the first light of dawn. He handed it to Julio proudly.

We stared in awe. In amazement. And some of us in silent fear.

Julio managed to smile through the haze of pain, blinking his eyes to stay awake. His fingers were laced tightly around the gun. He came toward me, walking like he was drunk, and pulled me into his arms. He wanted recognition. He wanted praise.

"Luz?"

I pretended to feel it, nodding and smiling as he threw his arms around me again. He held me tightly. And the gun's handle pressed into my side like an omen.

9:21 P.M.

When I close my eyes, I can still see him standing there in the park early that morning. Where it all began. I can see him holding on to that gun like it was his heart. Looking down at it, the silvery barrel and the handle. The trigger resting against his finger. Two weeks later, he used it for the first and last time.

3/2

WE MEET IN alleys piled high with trash. We meet in the shadows of abandoned tenements. Sometimes we meet in places that have no names. Location isn't important so long as the four of us are gathered together and ready to let go. It was Marty's idea, begun several months ago because once in a while—as he likes to say—we all need to bitch and beer.

When I got home from school today, I opened my bedroom door and found the little piece of paper sitting on the corner of my desk. Bram's handwriting, outlining the secret details:

B.B.S.
Time: 7:00 p.m.
Place: Classified
Attendance: Mandatory
(Keep it real.)

For the first time in days, I smiled. It was our secret code language. Marty had called one of our "meetings" on account of me. Felt good to know they were all concerned. We ate dinner and then told Sister Ellen we'd be taking our weekend recreation together. She gave me the okay to leave for a while. Asked us where we were going and I stumbled on my words for a minute. Thank God Marty is such an awesome liar. He jumped right in and told her we were headed to a poetry reading downtown. Don't know if Sister Ellen believed him, but she nodded and reminded us to be back by curfew.

We hit the streets and followed Marty's lead. Cold and windy outside. Traffic was backed up for blocks. Over by Third Avenue, we ducked into a small apartment building and stood for a minute in the entryway. Bram went to work picking the lock. In seconds we were inside the building, and Marty led us down a flight of stairs to a dark basement. Smelled dirty, like old drawers that haven't been opened in months. There was a little room off to the side, next to a humming boiler. We settled on the floor, got warm and then lit a candle. Marty took a forty of beer from his backpack that he'd bought from the bodega near the house. He uncapped it, took a sip. "The Bitch and Beer Society," he said. "Meeting's begun."

Before I could ask him anything, Bram took a pack of cigarettes from his jacket and lit one up. "So what's with you?" he said, looking straight into my eyes. "You got shit goin' on all around you, and we want you to *talk*."

I reached for the cigarette and took a deep drag. So nervous, my hands were trembling. I took a swig of the beer too. Silence. They were waiting for me to open up, but I've never known how to do that. Everything started racing through my brain, pictures of Julio and of Mickey Pesaturo. Pictures of me and the girl I used to be, the girl I swore I would never leave. It was too much to handle. The first tear dripped down my cheek. I cried silently. Couldn't bring myself to look up at them, so I cradled the bottle of beer like it was something sacred, like it would love me back if I held it tightly enough.

It was inevitable. Waiting to happen. I cried rivers for Julio when he died. Last month I cried because of Mickey Pesaturo.

But tonight, I cried for me. I let it all go. Just burst out with it, saying everything and holding nothing back. My fears. My anger. My confused little mind.

And if you cracked open my skull, this is what you would hear.

I'm afraid to talk about what happened the night Julio died.

I'm afraid that if I let go all the way, I'll never find my place in the world.

I'm afraid *not* to let go and move on because I don't wanna stay in this place.

I'm afraid that if I keep all this hate inside me, I'll never know how to love again.

I'm afraid that if I change too much, the kids back home will notice and think I've become someone weak. What'll they say about the gang girl who doesn't wanna fight anymore?

I'm afraid that all this rage inside will kill me.

I'm afraid that I'll end up like some of the girls from my old neighborhood—lost and depressed, or stuck in nowhere jobs, or pregnant but not married, or too tired to remember their dreams.

I'm afraid that I'll never get out of the inner city.

Feeling so guilty for admitting everything that way, but God, it felt good to get it out. To get it off my chest. To speak the truth.

Marty crawled over to me and wiped the tears from my face. The bruises on his cheeks were still so bad. He was hurting for me.

"I had no idea you felt that way," Bram said. "Shit, Luz—why didn't you ever say anything?"

Told him I was ashamed.

"Of what?" he snapped. "Admitting that you're human? You gotta lose that fucking problem." He stabbed his cigarette out on the floor and took a swig of the beer.

Clare told me I'll get through it. That I'm already on the right path. Marty said I have to start at the beginning and talk about what happened the night Julio died. I listened and felt all of it. Heard them too.

We made it back to the home just in time. We chewed cough drops all the way up 126th Street so our breath wouldn't smell like beer. Sister Ellen was waiting for us at the door, and I think she noticed the redness in my eyes when she saw me. Asked me if I was okay. I nodded, then went back to my room.

Late now. Quiet and dark. I'm calm. I'm cool. And I'm grateful for the last few hours and everything that happened, because now I know that sometimes it's okay to be scared. That sometimes you just have to burn up.

Michael T. Pesaturo
35 Carlton Road
Staten Island, NY 10329

March 4

Luz Cordero
St. Therese Home for Boys and Girls
105 West 135th Street
New York, NY 10037

Dear Luz,

    I know I'm the last person you ever expected
to get a letter from. I'm writing it hoping that
you'll read it all the way through and not crumple
it up. There are so many things I've wanted to say
to you in the last year and a half, but I kept
telling myself that it would be too tough, that you
wouldn't understand. I'm taking a chance now
not because I have to but because I want to.

    Seeing you that night in January was a sign
for me. It wasn't ever supposed to happen, but it
did. Something brought us face to face—a force, a
stroke of fate, God? I don't know. But standing
there, watching your face crumple at the sight of
me, was sobering.

    I'm not even sure where to start. Maybe I
should tell you a little about myself, the things you
might not know. I'm twenty-five years old and

I've been a cop for exactly two years. I grew up in the inner city too, in Brooklyn. My family was pretty poor. My dad is Italian, my mom Irish. I have three sisters. But wait—I'm getting off the point and I don't want to bore you.

This is what I'm trying to tell you: I think about the night Julio died all the time. I wake up and hear the gunshot. I fall asleep and dream of the blood. I had been a police officer for less than a year, and the last thing any cop wants to do is use his gun. You're probably rolling your eyes at this point because everyone just wants to believe that the NYPD is brutal, that we enjoy subjecting people to beatings and arrests and unnecessary force. But it's not true. That night, I never meant to open fire on Julio. You and I both know what happened. We both saw it. I know it's a painful memory, so I won't get into it. All I can say is that I'm not a bad person. I never meant to do what I did. The investigation was thorough, and justice, as they say, is blind when it comes to race, creed, sex, etc.

I know that Julio was your brother and that you loved him, but at the moment of death, when it's standing beside you and whispering in your ear, the line between stranger and loved one disappears and what you see is a fellow human being, a face like your own. A person who once shared all the same emotions and fears. You pull

the trigger because you don't want to lose your
own life, but in the end you lose it just the same.

Julio lost his heart, the physicality of being
alive. I lost my soul, the simple desire to go on
living.

That's what I've been thinking since that
night. That's what I've been feeling and shedding
tears over. All the rage you showed me as we stood
in that living room—I know what it's about. I've
thought about you a lot because I can't accept or
even imagine what I've taken from you. I'm sorry
for all of it. I'll be driving to work in the morning
and your face will flash in front of me, the way it
did in the newspapers and on television. The way
it did the night of the shooting. So much anger in
your eyes, but so much sadness too. And trust me,
Luz—I feel the same things. I became a cop
because I wanted to help people, to give back to
the community and the city and the neighborhood
where I was raised. It was never my intention to
inflict pain or do damage. If I could change
anything about my life, it would be the night Julio
died. The second time around, maybe I'd miss the
holster on my belt and grab the gun a fraction too
slowly. Maybe I'd turn around and allow death to
take me instead.

I'm sure all of this means nothing to you. I'm
writing on impulse, almost blindly, because seeing
you that night woke something up in me. It hit

too close to home. It made the reality all too real. In my heart, I guess I just don't want to accept that I've caused you so much pain.

I'm writing this letter in hopes that it'll bring you some peace. Maybe one day you'll write to me.

Mickey Pesaturo

3/7

MY HANDS HAVE been trembling since I got the letter. There was no return address on the envelope, so yesterday I opened it up thinking it was from my mom or one of the girls from the old neighborhood. Then his name jumped out at me. Reached up from the page and slammed me between the eyes.

Mickey Pesaturo. Writing me a letter.

I walked over to Sister Ellen's office and pushed open the door. Without saying anything, I held the letter out to her. Instead of shock, it was interest that showed on her face. She read every word, taking her sweet time, and then nodded to herself. I sat there and looked at her and couldn't speak. Freaking out. Feeling all strange inside. Scared. Annoyed. Nervous. *What does he want from me?*

Sister Ellen cut to the chase, telling me that I shouldn't start analyzing the letter. I should just respond to it and take action. She thinks it's proof that Mickey Pesaturo is hurting. That he was affected by seeing me. Bram agrees with her. So do Marty and Clare. Everyone has an opinion but me.

Simple, they said. No problem. Just do it.

Yeah, right.

Didn't sleep at all last night. I had stuffed the letter to the back of my desk drawer, not wanting to see it or be reminded of it. But then, past midnight, I got up and pulled it out. Read it again and again. I'm still sitting on the same question—why? After the way I acted when he came here, why would Mickey Pesaturo wanna contact me, or hear from me? To talk about Julio? About the night he died?

I keep flashing back to Sister Ellen's words. Yesterday, she asked me flat out if I wanna live the rest of my life in the shadow of Julio's death.

No, I don't. That's the honest answer. The answer I couldn't give her, or myself, until now. When Julio died, I thought I would suffer for the rest of my life because it was a way of paying him respect. A way of never forgetting. Now I know that I can't go on like this. It's killing me.

Feel like a fucking hypocrite writing this. Just a few weeks ago I would've taken Mickey Pesaturo's letter and set it to a match because the thought of him made me sick. I never expected to hear from him like this. Never expected to see his own words reflecting a part of him that's human. Does that make sense?

I'm thinking about the night of our Bitch and Beer meeting. How I cried. How I let it all out. Something changed. Shifted. Rocked. It was like I left my own skin for a little while and saw myself from a different place. A strange light passed over me. Letting it all out felt good, and for the first time, I didn't try to take it back or convince anyone that I was lying. Back in the Bronx, the girls from my crew would've flipped out if they'd heard me crying and admitting so many things. And they'd probably skin my ass right now if they knew I was thinking about a letter a cop wrote me.

A cop. The one who killed my brother.

I just wrote that sentence. And I can look at it, feel it and still hold on to my emotions. Couldn't say that a few weeks ago.

I don't know what any of it means. I'm sitting here at my desk staring at Mickey Pesaturo's letter. Staying calm. Confused but cool.

It's kinda like a new wound—hurts a little, but the pain is something I can handle. So, for now, I'm just gonna let it bleed.

3/9

IN FIRST PERIOD. History. Wish I wasn't here.

So. Anyway.

I reread the letter this morning. Kept staring down at Mickey Pesaturo's name right there on the page. It was a little easier this time. Didn't feel as nervous and edgy skimming over his words and his handwriting. Some of what he wrote is true. Or maybe I should say that I understand it—the emotion, the pain.

And sitting here, I'm wondering . . . What would've happened if I hadn't gone crazy that night when he showed up at the house? If I'd handled it differently, stayed calm and spoken to him, would I be in a different place now?

All these questions and no easy answers. I just need time. I need to step away from it before I can get close, ya know?

3/14

HUNG OUT WITH Marty tonight. After dinner we headed outside, just the two of us. I didn't know where he was taking me, but I followed his lead. We walked down 126th Street and then over to Third Avenue. Chilly, but there was still light at five-thirty. Reminded me that spring is coming, that it's been well over a month since I saw Mickey Pesaturo in the living room of the house. And it was Marty who reminded me that a lot's changed since then. We didn't talk about the letter, and I'm glad. We got close, the two of us, huddling against the chill until we reached the shadowy strip of Hunts Point Avenue in the South Bronx.

Hunts Point. What we used to call Blood Row.

It'd been over a year since I'd walked on those streets. Last time I hung out by the warehouses, there was a shoot-out because a gang from the Lower East Side had invaded dangerous turf. Being there tonight spooked me a little. But Marty told me to relax and that nothing was gonna happen. As we got deeper into the maze of streets, he knew his way around. Like he'd been there before a couple of times. And he had.

"You ever wonder about the people who work here?" he asked me.

Shook my head. Then I realized what he was talking about when I saw a young girl step out of the shadows. Probably a few years older than me, like maybe twenty, dressed in a thin little skirt and a tattered jacket. Tits half hanging out, lips and eyes done up with color. She ran out onto the street as a car pulled up. The headlights blinded me for a second, but I saw her lean into the window and then get inside.

Made me feel sick. I wondered what she'd have to do to earn a few dollars, and as the car sped away, I wondered whether she'd come back alive.

We walked another block, past one of the big deserted warehouses. The wind blew, smelling like smoke. That's when I spotted the other hustlers, the young guys in jeans and sweaters waiting for the horny truck drivers to show up. One of the guys looked straight at us, meeting my eyes. He couldn't have been eighteen. Thought he was gonna snap at me when his thin lips cracked into a smile and he said, "Hey, Marty! What up?"

Marty smiled. He swung the backpack from his shoulders and opened it up. Inside were a bunch of soup cans and candy bars from the house. "How's it going, Allen?"

They knew each other. Shook hands, joked around. Allen nodded at me. He took one of the candy bars from Marty like it was cash, tore it open and started eating. Then he asked Marty how everything was going at St. Therese, if he was okay and pulling through. Marty said, "Yeah, it's cool," and threw his glance further down the street. There were about six or seven other guys doing the rounds. They all knew Marty. Called his name, thanked him when he gave them the cans and the candy. Like a reunion of worn-out souls.

I tried not to think about the fact that Marty used to haunt these streets with the rest of them, selling himself for food or drugs.

He kept glancing sideways at me as the other guys chatted him up, maybe wondering if I was shocked or disgusted or disappointed. That look of fear in his eyes like he had at school when he sat in the cafeteria, afraid someone was gonna call him a faggot or threaten to kick his ass. But I just shook my head at him and touched his arm.

"The streets," I told him, "are all I know. The streets, and what people do to survive on them, are cool with me."

When the food was gone and headlights flooded the darkness, the guys slipped back onto the sidewalk and went to work. Marty lit a cigarette. We sat down on the curb and froze our asses off, listening as car doors opened and slammed shut.

How much, kid?

Forty bucks.

Marty turned his eyes away from me. I took two puffs of the cigarette, then said, "How long were you here?"

"Too long," he said. And then he told me. He hustled for about seven months, on and off. It was after he ran away from home the seventh time. Lived with his mother in Brooklyn, but all his life she had guys in and out of the house. A boozer, he said. She never cared for him. Neither did any of her boyfriends. Once, when he was ten, she beat Marty so bad that social services came and put him in foster care for three months. Then he went back to her. It wasn't any good. He kept running away, and she kept telling him she didn't give a shit. The day he told his mother that he liked guys, she freaked out and tried beating him again. But she didn't get too far, because Marty defended himself and hit back. That night he left home for good. He found his way to the streets, did what he had to do to survive. When he got arrested for soliciting an undercover cop, social services contacted his mother, but she didn't want anything to do with him. The streets can keep the faggot, she said. She didn't care if he was alive or dead. It was the last time he ever heard from her. A few weeks later, he came to St. Therese.

I huddled close to him as it got colder. So much was running through my mind, but I finally asked him the one question that I'd been asking myself: "If you could go back and change one thing about your life, what would it be?"

Marty stood up and swung the backpack onto his shoulders. He didn't look at me, but he said, "If I could go back to the day I left home for the last time, I would tell my mother that I love her."

Not because he thought it would have changed the situation, he told me, but because it would've changed *him*. His life and his mind and his heart. Even after all the shit he'd been through, saying those words to his mother would've made him stronger, and they would've let him put the past away. Instead, he's had to learn how to do that the hard way.

The whole way home, I thought about what he'd said. Now I'm sitting in my room, listening to the voices and the cars pass by on the street. Same old thing outside.

But here, inside me, nothing is the same.

It's the way I see things, how I feel about them now. Less anger. Nothing's like it used to be, and that's the strangest thing. When did it happen? Was it the night I saw Mickey Pesaturo? The days after the fight at school? I don't know. In a crazy, fucked-up way, holding that letter in my hands makes me feel stronger, like if I can read his words and know what's going on in his head, maybe I can handle a lot more. Maybe I can look back and see what I've done wrong too.

ME

you say it's an answer
I say it's a question
I give you examples
you give me suggestions
you can pray all you want
on your knobby knee
but it's not about you
and it ends with me
yeah I wanna be good
wanna find the strong girl
but whenever I try
the gates unfurl
I know I've got it in me
I'm a goddess in the dark
touch my soul and
you'll see a spark
open your mouth and
spin me a rhyme
I'll show you that
confusion
ain't a crime
you got the time?

then stand in line
don't mess with my head
and we'll be just fine

I can't be a saint
already failed that test
I've played with sin
just like the rest
I'm real
I'm here
I know what to do
but it ain't as easy as
two plus two
yeah that's right
I'm talkin' to you
so listen up
you hear me, boo?
lemme spell it out
it's not an equation
you're the border and
I'm the nation
you're talkin' peace
I'm under occupation
so what's better?
isolation?
oh fuck that
I need a relation
a station
without limitation

another minute before
I begin my invasion
and then we can rise to
the sweet occasion

there's so much drama
the world don't care
this is our fight and
I'm takin' the dare
this is our story so
I'll see you there

3/19

SAW ANNE BURNS today. She met me in front of the building instead of in her office. I was cold after walking the long blocks from school, and when she saw me, she put up her hand and hailed a cab. I asked her where we were going. She told me to just get in and relax.

We sat side by side in the cab. It sped across South Street and over the Brooklyn Bridge. Dusk was falling. I stared across the water at the lights of the city as they twinkled and then faded into nothingness. When the cab came to a stop, we got out in front of a small park. It was fenced in, kind of messy looking, with trash on the sidewalk and pieces of plywood thrown over the ground. I hadn't been to Williamsburg in a long time. But then I remembered that it's Anne's neighborhood, the place where she grew up. Told me once that she got her ass kicked on Classon Avenue when she was fifteen.

I followed her past the fences and into the park. We walked around the short bushes, the bent trees, and came to the back wall, where a different world opened up before my eyes. Graffiti everywhere, the kind that makes sense, and about a dozen paintings and sketches glowing under the indigo sky. So incredible, it took my breath away. I looked at the pictures, at the faces and the words and the little angels that had been drawn in the corners. It was a memory wall.

JOHNNY HILDAGO R.I.P.
SAMANTHA GRAY IN OUR HEARTS
PETER VELASQUEZ WITH GOD

Different names, all of them bound together in death. There was a tombstone in the middle of the wall, painted black but colored with pink roses and clouds. Posthumous art. On the left side, just above a broken fountain, was a list of dates. Young lives, all of them.

I looked at Anne. "How did they die?"

"Some of the names are already ten years old," she said. "Some of them were added last month. They all died young, and violently. Gang wars, shootings, stabbings, robberies, suicides. Whatever. The point of the wall is to show that they'll always be remembered, no matter what."

I watched as Anne put her shoulder bag down on a rotting bench. She opened it up and took out a thermos, then poured some coffee into the small cup.

"Here," she said. "It'll warm you up."

I sat down beside her. The coffee was good, but I was itching for a cigarette. I was about to reach into my backpack when Anne handed me her pack of Newports and a lighter.

"You didn't get those from me, kid."

"Deal." I lit up.

She put a cigarette in her mouth and looked at me. Then she said, "I hear it's been a tough couple of weeks at St. Therese. Sister Ellen tells me you haven't been talking much, or even leaving your room after school."

I sipped the coffee. Didn't say anything.

Anne jabbed a finger into my shoulder. "I don't blame you for freaking out with everything that's been going on in your life," she said. "It's a lot to deal with." She puffed hard on her own cigarette, and I felt okay with the silence between us. Then she asked me about the letter. Not about how it made me feel, but about what I'm gonna do about it. Write Mickey Pesaturo back? Meet with him?

I couldn't answer her straight up, so I told her what I'd been wanting to tell her for a long time. "I'm feeling a lot better," I said. "Stronger."

A smirk lit up her face. "I know that," she whispered. "You have that power inside you, Luz."

I looked down and asked her for a pen. I wanted to write Julio's name on that wall so that he'd be remembered like all the rest. But then Anne walked over to the right side of the wall and bent down, squatting on her heels. She motioned me over and pointed to a small square section of the colored concrete.

It read:

JULIO CORDERO

R.I.P.

My eyes got wide. Further down was the date he had died, all of it sketched in light blue and orange. "You did that?" I asked Anne.

"Not a chance," she said. "This is somebody else's work. When I first saw it a few months ago, I thought maybe you had done it, but then I remembered that you didn't know Brooklyn all that well."

My eyes were locked on his name, the letters and the date. Stunned. Told her that it was probably one of Julio's friends from the old neighborhood.

But Anne shook her head. She pointed to a little spot below Julio's name, and I saw close-up that three numbers had been etched into the concrete. 4-2-7.

"The last three numbers of Mickey Pesaturo's badge," she said. "He's the one who remembered Julio here, Luz."

I didn't move as her words hit me. I didn't even feel the cold wind or hear the traffic honking on the street.

Anne said she knows for a fact that it was him. Maybe last year, maybe last month. She said it didn't matter because the point was clear. Mickey Pesaturo's been thinking about Julio the same way I have. "I want you to know that," she said. "I want you to believe it."

I'm still stunned. It's been hours since I got back home, but the shock hasn't gone away. Standing at that wall, I ran my fingers over the sketching of Julio's name, then over the numbers of Mickey Pesaturo's badge. Such a weird feeling. Like we were together, all three of us, for the second time. But this time there weren't any shots. There wasn't any blood.

And I wasn't crying.

3/22

Dear Julio,

Wherever you are, I know you're hearing this. You can see that I'm confused, going out of my skull. Nothing makes sense anymore. There's so much I need to tell you, but starting is like swimming across the ocean: impossible.

Getting the letter from Mickey Pesaturo spooked me. If it had arrived last year, I probably would've shredded it with a butcher knife, but now things are different. I hate admitting the truth, and the truth is that I've changed. I still mourn you every day. I still think of you and remember how much you loved me. But I'm not sure my heart can take the craziness of this fight.

Please don't be angry with what I have to say.

The thing is, so many people have lost people they love, and just as violently. I read about them in magazines and see them on TV. I hear about them in therapy. They have pain, and yet there comes a point when they understand that nothing can change the past and that life continues. This doesn't mean forgetting. I think it means accepting. I never thought I'd wanna reach that point, because my rage has always been so strong, like a separate heart beating in sync with my own. But you see, I really do wanna find some peace, and I can only do that if I let go a little.

I feel so guilty writing it. I remember how much you resented the cops, even when we were kids. How you used to look at them and say they were the enemy. All the blacks and Puerto Ricans in the neighborhood thought so, and I guess you followed suit. The inner city never gave us a chance to escape the mediocrity, and people did what they had to do to survive. Even you. So whenever we saw our neighbors getting arrested for selling drugs or stealing from the grocery store, you would rant about the injustice of it all, of how the cops pinpointed minorities and not white people. You hated the boys in blue. And all this time, I've been keeping up the same fight because I wanted to make you proud. I wanted justice too, but in truth, I've been telling myself that accepting you're gone and moving on would somehow dishonor your memory. The fear of abandoning you, even in death, has caged me. I live in a windowless room and the darkness is scaring me. I need some light, and I can only find it if I try to move on.

The fears are still inside me. Mostly, I'm afraid that I'll find new strength and that it'll eclipse the girl I used to be. Back in the old neighborhood, when I was in the gang, we all *made a promise to keep our identities as fighters. So I've been walking around thinking that I have to live this life of battles and struggles because of where I come from and what I look like. I've been fighting like a thug because I never thought I'd be capable of anything else. Now I believe differently.*

The past year, living at St. Therese, has chipped away at the cement in my soul. I don't wanna admit it, but I think maybe, with each new day, the girl I used to be is dying little by little. And if I'm willing to put her to rest, I have to do the same for you.

Don't hate me for feeling this way, Julio. I'll never forget my blood, or yours. This isn't even about you. It's really a way of growing up and coming to terms with my world. Maybe not every cop is bad. Maybe a girl from the inner city can make it past the prejudice and the stereotypes and be okay.

Maybe that girl is me?

3/26

NIGHT. MAYBE SIX o'clock. Maybe ten o'clock.
Don't know. I've lost track of time in the craziness of
it all.

The strangeness of it all . . .

I asked Sister Ellen to make a phone call for me
today. She got in touch with Mickey Pesaturo, and he
agreed to a meeting. We're gonna see each other face
to face, right here in the living room, in five days.

3/28

they say my name is Hope
a heart that keeps on beating
they think I'll get past the wounds
and finally stop the bleeding—
a girl walking out of the fire
coming slowly into the rain
she's burned but the ashes are glowing
is that the miracle of pain?

I think my name is Maybe
or Gimme-a-Minute-to-Chill
the puzzle is still in pieces
but the picture is no longer still—
I'm standing on the edge of reason
forgetting the shouts and cries
because something inside of you lives
when the person inside of you dies
something inside of you swims
when the water starts to rise

3/30

BRAM PERFORMED AT Grand Central today. After school, he headed uptown with his violin case and asked me if I wanted to join him. Had nothing better to do, so I tagged along. I think he likes it when someone goes with him. Makes him feel less self-conscious. When we got there, rush hour was just starting and trains were roaring off the platforms. People pushed and shoved. The usual chaos. He found an empty space against the wall and opened the case, leaving it by his feet for the people who decided to chuck us some change. I sat close to him, trying to blend in. Stupid me. I had no instrument—just a scared face and nothing to say.

Bram looked at me and asked if there was anything I wanted to hear. He said, "How about something calm for a change? You look like shit." I flipped him the finger, then listened as he started to play. So beautiful. A slow, powerful piece. A sonata, he said. Mozart. I'd never heard it before. He said he'd been working with a lot of classical stuff in music lab at school. As he played, holding the violin up against his chin, he said, "Close your eyes. Think. Let go."

I gave it a shot. Squeezed my lids shut and let the

music take me away. Felt like I was drifting off for a few seconds, moving into a calm, quiet place. All the tension inside me disappeared. I stayed like that for a while, just me and the nothingness. The peace. Now I know what Bram means when he talks about losing himself in the mad music. How it heals him. He knew I needed some of that.

In minutes people started gathering around us. Old and young. Black and white. Men in business suits and women with their kids. All eyes on Bram. He got more into it, burning across those strings like a wildfire. Sweat beaded his forehead. His dreads whipped against his face and his skin got red with heat. I watched as coins fell and dollar bills floated down into the open case. And when he finished, applause.

He totally amazed me today. He made me feel, if only for a little bit, like everything was okay. Peaceful. At ease. But when I told him that, he shook his head and said, "Bullshit. You felt that way because you wanted to feel it. You're ready for a little peace and calm."

Yeah, I am. But I'm also stressed-out fucked-up mad nervous! Can't stop thinking about tomorrow. Bram said he'd play his violin in the hallway all night long if it meant keeping me calm, and he just might have to.

3/31

DAWN. I'M STARING out the window, watching the sun streak the horizon. The sky is pink. The wind is cool.

Didn't sleep all night. Tossed and turned and even prayed a little.

Today is the day. Today, I'm meeting with Mickey Pesaturo.

Seems like the whole house is in a state of suspense. A little while ago, Marty smuggled an extra handful of cigarettes upstairs. Clare came into my room when it was still dark—she knew I wasn't sleeping. We sat on the bed and just hung out.

She asked me if I was scared.

And I admitted it—I'm petrified.

I guess Mickey Pesaturo is too. Neither of us knows what to expect. But no matter what happens, I know this is the right thing to do. The best decision.

So listen . . . I'm gonna try to get some rest, maybe eat something. I don't know when I'll be able to write again, but I will eventually. All depends on how this meeting goes and how I feel afterward.

Wish me luck.

✳   ✳   ✳

He was standing in the living room when I went downstairs. I paused, took a deep breath and studied him. Mickey Pesaturo is of average height. He has a strong worked-out body and a lot of brown hair. Looks a little older than he is because of the goatee. He was wearing jeans and a white shirt. Pale in the daylight. I had never noticed the way his eyes twitched when he glanced around.

Sister Ellen was sitting on the couch. She saw me and stood up.

I walked over to them. There was a hush, but then I heard the blood rushing in my ears. Felt dizzy when Mickey set his eyes on me.

He said, "Hi."

I froze on the spot, staring. I cleared my throat. "Hi," I answered.

Sister Ellen motioned to the couch and the chair beside it. She had set a tray on the coffee table: bottled water, soda, crackers and cookies.

Mickey Pesaturo lowered himself into one corner of the couch, and I went for the chair, a little further away from him. Thought Sister Ellen was gonna sit too, but she only nodded at me. I looked at her with desperation. She put a hand on my shoulder, patted it. Then she left the room and the door closed behind her.

Just the two of us, sitting there: Mickey Pesaturo and me. It was such a strange feeling, nothing to convey in words. The weirdness of it all. For a minute I thought that that would be the extent of it, that we'd sit there and listen to traffic drift by.

And then he spoke. "Thanks for reading my letter, Luz. I really appreciate it."

For the first time, I stared at him. I mean, I took him in completely, seeing the glassy sheen of his eyes and the dark circles beneath. Close up, he somehow resembled a bruised little kid. I saw his age in that moment. Twenty-five. Only eight years older than me. He hadn't looked this way the night Julio died. They kept flashing in front of me, those images, but I forced them away. And when the twinge of anger rose up, I all but punched it out of my heart.

"I bet you were surprised hearing from me like that," he said.

Told him I was. That I'd never expected it.

"That night, when I came here with the other two officers—it was just such a powerful experience, ya know? I had no idea this was where you were living."

"For a year now," I told him.

He nodded. "So, then . . . you had to come live here after . . ." His voice was deep and slow, and it trailed off as he touched the raw nerve between us. He wanted to say *after your brother died and your family fell apart,* but he didn't.

"Yeah," I said. "This is where I came."

"I'm sorry."

The words steeled me. "For what?" I asked him.

"Well . . . for everything," he answered. He hung his head and took a deep breath. Then he looked up at me again. "For what happened the night your brother died. For the fact that you have to live here. For all the pain you're feeling. That's really what I came here to say. I know it might not mean anything to you right now, but it's the truth. I'm sorry, Luz."

"It means something," I muttered.

"It does?"

"Well . . . yeah."

He nodded slowly, trying to understand my point.

I was trying to understand it too. Not that I felt forgiveness—I didn't. The emotions clutching me had more to do with a sense of justice, of getting even. I could see that he was pained and that he suffered because of his actions. Couldn't help noticing it. And for some reason, that made me feel better. Less alone. It was like a little touch of revenge, the kind that you don't inflict but hear about after the fact, like when the mean kid at school breaks his arm falling down a flight of stairs. *Good, you deserve to cry too.*

I reached for the can of soda on the table, popped the cap and guzzled it down.

Mickey Pesaturo drank some water. He was nervous and fidgety, folding and unfolding his hands, leaning back and then forward. He said, "I live over on Staten Island. But I work at the precinct down by Hudson Street. I do a lot of safety talks and demonstrations all over the city. That's why I ended up coming here. I don't patrol anymore."

"Do you ever think about him?" The question escaped my lips before I could even consider it.

He knew what I meant. His eyes widened a little. "Yes," he said. "I think about Julio a lot. And I think about you. Everything I said in my letter is true." A pause. "I was honest. I want you to be too. You can say to me whatever's on your mind."

"It's just hard for me to sympathize with you," I told him. "I mean, you killed him. You raised that gun and pulled the trigger and–" Stopped myself right there. A tremble in my voice. Knew I was headed for trouble, so I just let it go.

He was silent, waiting.

A dog barked somewhere across the street.

"Sorry," I mumbled.

"Don't be. Please. This is what I want. I want you to be honest, even if it means screaming and yelling at me, calling me names. Whatever. That's why I came."

But I told him I wouldn't do that. I wasn't gonna sit there and hurl shit at him, because I'd spent the last year and a half acting like that. I didn't wanna be that person anymore.

"I understand," he said.

"No, you don't," I snapped. "I don't expect you to understand because no one can. Stop trying to make it sound like you do. We have different types of pain. We're not on the same level just because we have a dead person in common."

It was coming outta me fast. Felt good, though. My words hit him hard and he was staring at the floor. Strands of hair fell over his forehead. I couldn't see his eyes.

He said, "Do you want to talk about the night Julio died?"

"No."

"Can I tell you what I did after they took him away in the ambulance?"

I didn't answer. He took my silence as a yes.

"I sat in the back of the police cruiser for about an hour," Mickey Pesaturo began. "There were a bunch of other cops with me. I was shaken up. I couldn't believe what had happened. I had never fired my gun before, so I was really in shock. One of the guys drove me back to the precinct and I stood there for a while, answering questions and trying to put everything together. . . ."

But it was all too much for him. He said he couldn't deal with the weight of what had happened: the sight of Julio lying there, me kneeling down beside him with blood on my palms and tears staining my cheeks. The way I screamed. That night, Mickey Pesaturo left the precinct and walked the two miles to Jacobi Medical Center, even though the other cops told him not to.

"On the way there, I pulled off my badge and my uniform pins," he went on. "I stuffed everything in my pockets because I didn't want to look like a cop. By the time I got to the hospital, there were about a dozen reporters in the lobby. I sneaked in through the emergency room and started asking questions, and one of the nurses told me that Julio had died of his wounds. I started sobbing. I kept telling her that maybe she'd made a mistake. I couldn't accept that I might be responsible for some-one else's death. And the fact that Julio was only a couple of years younger than me at the time . . . it was too much. When I finally calmed down, I asked where you were."

They didn't tell him. They didn't even know. No one knew, because I had busted out of the emer-gency room the moment the doctor officially pro-nounced Julio dead. I ran past the security guards and the nurses. Past the reporters. I flew into one of the stairways and climbed. Kept climbing until my lungs burned and my feet throbbed. A mess of a per-son. Soaked in blood, smelling like puke. I left red handprints on the walls when I tried to steady my-self against the dizziness. Finally I made it up to the rooftop, thinking that if I climbed high enough I would somehow be able to reach my brother—touch his face, hear his voice. It didn't happen. Stood there, balancing myself against the ledge, looking down at the street. Above me, a helicopter beat the humid air.

"I don't know what made me go into the stairwell," Mickey went on. "It was just a feeling, a hunch. I kept going and then I saw the blood and knew you had been there. I made it to the roof. I looked through the doorway and saw you there. I'll never forget the way you were doubled over, grabbing at your knees. You were crying so hard. I swear, Luz, I stood a few feet away, invisible, crying too. I wanted more than anything to approach you and say something."

Instead, he'd turned and made his way back down to the lobby.

He was telling the truth. I know for sure because I've never uttered a word about that night to anyone. Isn't a single soul out there who saw me on the rooftop of Jacobi Medical Center. That was the first time I cried after Julio died. Alone. Closed off from the world. Too tough to admit that I had tears in me like every other person.

But he was there. Mickey Pesaturo.

My enemy.

And the only human being to witness what I'd always believed was an intimate, personal moment.

I said, "What did you do after you left the hospital?"

"I went home and cried some more," he told me. "And then I spent the next six months falling apart."

"But you're still a cop," I said. "How do you go out there every day and not worry about something like this happening again?"

"I do worry," he said. "I hear that gunshot all the time. But I don't patrol the streets anymore. It was a condition of the investigation that I do desk duty and other things. I can't work the streets anymore." He paused, looked down at his hands. "You know, after the grand jury cleared me of all charges and I went back to work, everyone told me to just sit down and accept the desk job because they didn't think I'd ever be able to hold a gun and defend the way a cop has to. I never wanted to believe that, but sometimes I do."

Asked him if he was in therapy, like me.

He nodded. "Yeah, of course. Twice a week. But, you know, sometimes doctors just can't heal you. Sometimes you have to go about finding ways to heal yourself."

His way of telling me what this meeting was all about, I guess.

The awkwardness between us didn't leave. I felt it with every ticking moment. But in a way it was good because it gave me a chance to really absorb this guy, this walking wreck who had killed my brother. I mean, I didn't see an angel sitting there

across from me, but I know I saw something new—
something I'd never seen before, not even in the
newspaper photos of him. And I also saw something
familiar in his eyes—the way they moved, the con-
stant searching of a single space. Mine do the same
thing. When your mind is desperate you can't help
seeking every damn crevice for a sign that might explain what you're feeling.

My heart had stopped slamming. I was a little
more relaxed.

"Is there anything you want to ask, or say to
me?" There was a trace of fear in his voice.

I asked him what his days were like. Did he go
out with his friends after work? And the nights. Did
he watch TV and listen to music and just chill? I had
to know, because I'd always had this vision of him
living a normal, ordinary life, without any of the shit
I go through.

He laughed at that. "Well, I go to my shrink twice
a week, and after that I don't feel much like doing
anything. Usually after work on the other nights I go
running down by the river. If I'm off during the day,
I usually read or work out."

He took in the walls, all the statues of Jesus and
the Virgin Mary and the Crucifixion. His eyes froze
on the picture above the mantel, the one of St.
Therese holding a blood red rose.

*Is he religious? Does he pray and believe in an after-
life? What about forgiveness from God? If he has that,*

what do I matter? I wanted to know, but I let the silence fill up the space between us.

He felt it too, the tension. He looked at his watch and stood. "I guess I've taken up a lot of your time," he said.

And when I didn't say anything back, we walked out of the living room and into the hallway.

Mickey Pesaturo was at the front door. He stared at me. Said, "I know it would be hard for you, but the precinct where I work holds meetings every week for cops and members of the community—for people who've lost loved ones and for cops who were involved. If you ever wanna come, just let me know." He took the folded edge of a piece of paper from his jacket pocket and handed it to me.

I glanced down at the words on it: *Speak: A Forum for the Inner City.*

"Thank you again," he said. Then he shut the door and was gone.

I stood there for a long time in the semidarkness. Dusk was falling. I listened as the "Salve Regina" started playing through the house, as calm and cool and cautious as the beating of my heart.

4/1

THIS IS HOW it was, and this is what I said:

That night. A few hours after Julio's death. A haze of tears and shock. Anger. At the hospital, the detectives from the Forty-third Precinct found me on my way down from the roof and silently ushered me outside and into a waiting police cruiser. And twenty minutes later, into a small hot interrogation room.

They sat me down and brought me water. One of the female cops, a black lady with long red nails and sweet eyes, wet a paper towel and dragged it across my face. There was blood on my cheeks. Two other detectives stood over me. They set a tape recorder on the table and pressed the Record button.

"Please state your name and age," one of them said.

"Luz Cordero. I'm sixteen."

"Where were you at about nine o'clock to-night, Luz?"

I shook my head. Couldn't remember.

One of the male cops pushed the cup of water toward me and said, "Were you hanging out with your friends in front of the candy store on Zerega Avenue?"

I nodded. "Yeah."

"And did you see your brother, Julio Cordero, come out of your apartment building?"

"Yeah."

"Did he say anything to you?"

Silence. I closed my eyes and trembled, remembering his last words. Hearing his voice in my mind. "No," I whispered. "He didn't say anything to me."

"Nothing at all? You didn't approach him?"

"No."

They made notes in their pads. I stared up at the lightbulb on the ceiling; it was blinking.

The cop cleared his throat. "Did you see Julio get into his car and leave?"

"I think so. I don't remember."

The female cop nudged my hand gently. "Try to think, sweetie. Think real hard. Was he with anyone? Did you see him get into his car?"

"No."

"What did you do after he left?" the male detective asked.

"I don't remember."

"What made you walk up Zerega Avenue and to the warehouses? It's deserted there at night."

I didn't answer.

"Luz?"

"I felt like walking," I said.

"Were you going to look for Julio?"

"I didn't know where he was going."

The cops all exchanged looks, then scrawled on their pads again.

"Luz, your brother was shot in the empty parking lot behind the hat factory. When the police cars and ambulances arrived, they found you kneeling beside him. What did you see in the moments before he was shot?"

"I didn't see anything. I was just walking."

"You heard the shot?"

"Yeah."

"Where were you when you heard the shot?"

I fingered the cup of water. It kept echoing in my head—that shot. The loud boom. "I don't remember. I was close to the parking lot, I guess."

"And what did you see?"

"Nothing."

One of the male detectives pulled out a chair and sat down across from me. "You must've seen something, Luz. Did you see the first police cruiser pull into the parking lot and Officer Mickey Pesaturo get out of the car?"

"No."

"You never saw the first police cruiser? You never saw Officer Pesaturo?"

"I saw him later, after I saw Julio lying on the ground."

"Okay, so you get to the parking lot after you hear the shot, and then you see Julio lying on the ground, right?"

"Yeah."

"And then?"

I squeezed my eyes shut. Tears spilled over my cheeks.

They waited, silently, for me to speak.

"I ran over to him," I said. "I started touching his face. He was already dead, I think."

"Where was Officer Pesaturo?"

"I don't know. Standing over by the car, I think. I don't know. That's all I saw. Julio was already dead. He had already been killed."

"So you're saying you didn't see what happened before Julio was shot, right?"

"Right," I whispered.

"You're saying you never saw Officer Pesaturo approach Julio. You never saw or heard them exchange words or argue?"

"He killed my brother," I said, choking on the words.

"How d'you know? You saw Officer Pesaturo shoot Julio? You saw him pull the trigger?"

I wiped my eyes. I was breathing hard. I looked up into the cop's face and said, "Who else could've killed him? That cop is a liar. He stood there and shot my brother for no reason!"

The female cop put her hands on my shoulders and held me in the chair.

I sat still. I looked into their cold faces and shook my head. And I knew then and there that it was a war, that Julio was just another casualty, and that I didn't matter to them. It was black and white. It was politics and red tape. "You want me to say that I witnessed everything," I snapped. "And that I saw Officer Pesaturo defending himself, or some bullshit like that, right? That's what you want. It's easier to believe that than it is to hear that a big and mighty cop shot a dumb spic from the streets in cold blood, right?"

The detective shook his head. "We're just trying to piece together the events as they happened, Luz."

"I told you what happened. My brother didn't have to die."

"Officer Pesaturo is a good cop. He's in good standing and it's hard for us to believe that he shot your brother intentionally or–"

"Well, fuck you," I spat. "I don't give a shit what you think. And I'm not gonna lie just so you can sweep Julio's death under the rug. I know what happened."

The detective stood up. "I know you do, Luz. And I'm hoping that one day soon, one day very soon, you'll tell us the truth."

I turned my face away from him. The black female cop led me out of the room and into the bustling precinct corridor. Reporters were milling around outside. Cameras flashed and sirens were going off, and everything I had ever known or be-lieved dissolved into the air. Into nothingness. Alone in the world, I became my own army.

My life was over. My life had just begun.

4/7

I WANTED TO do it. My idea. Something like this—a moment in life so powerful—deserves to be *marked*.

Saturday. A cool windy night. Alone in the living room right now, letting the pain do its thing. Feeling good.

Early this morning I caught Bram leaving his room, violin snagged on his shoulder. He was wearing short sleeves. I knew what that meant and asked him if we could chill together. He said, "I'm not sure you wanna come with me today." I nodded and told him that yeah, I did. I understood. It was one of his secret days, when he disappears till nightfall and comes back smiling. We took the subway to Queens, to a little banged-up house in Ozone Park, and when we got there I met his other friends. The freaky circle, as he put it.

I'd seen them in school—Pete, Chris, Jerome and Shelly. They're all like Bram. Pete's half white and half black, with light skin and kinky hair. Chris's mother is Chinese, his father Spanish. Jerome's black, but he's got bright blue eyes and his white mother's features. Shelly's a mix of everything— Indian, Dominican, a little white and Asian. They were all standing in the garage of the house—Pete's house—when we got there. Bram didn't know what to say at first. The others all looked at me like they were disappointed, like I'd broken their secret code. Couldn't blame them. I look Puerto Rican, plain and simple. Not much mystery to me. So when the silence in the room became too much, Bram introduced me and said, "Luz is cool. She knows the bad story like we do."

Shelly came up to me first. Smiled and told me that what I'd been through was rough, and that how I'd been handling it was admirable. Pete and Jerome said the same thing. Chris told me that he'd seen me the day of the fight at school and that he'd been scared of me ever since.

"I'm better now," I said.

Chris threw a glance at Bram. "Yeah," he answered. "I know."

Bram had told them all about me, so to them it didn't matter that I had only one race in me. They still saw me as a part of the circle because I knew what it meant to be rejected, and hurt, and angry. Fighting and hurting, and then facing your fears—that makes someone a freak because not many people have the guts to do it.

I took a seat in a corner of the garage and listened as they started to jam. Bram played his violin. Chris was on bass, Pete on guitar. Shelly's a little madwoman with the drums. They got into it, making their own music and losing themselves in the process. Different rhythms. Different sounds. But all the same soul. Then Bram set my words to the music. . . .

Kids dying and mothers crying
and my dreams are bright with pain . . .

For the first time in a while, I didn't think about other things. I just sat there and stayed in the moment, calm and cool. When they finished up, I went to Bram's side and touched the tattoo on his shoulder. A snake. There's a star on his arm too. Told him that I wanted to mark myself, that I wanted to seal everything that's happened on my skin. Permanently.

It's for me, my own little cut. My way of coloring the void.

It was Pete who did it. He's got the tools right there in his garage. Makes money giving tattoos to the kids at school, but today he worked for free. I sat down in a cushioned chair and watched as he fired up his tray. The ink gun, the pads, the alcohol. I unbuttoned my shirt and pulled it over my head. Shelly came and stood next to me as Bram, Jerome and Chris watched. My heart sped up. Hands shook a little. But Pete went easy on me, telling me to look away as he swiped alcohol over my left breast, right above my heart, where I wanted the tattoo. Shelly lit a cigarette and I think it was Bram who found the beer. I took a few sips and then settled in. There was only a little pain, nothing I couldn't stand. A quick nick, then a shiver. But I wanted it. Needed to feel it and conquer it. Sat there and let it all bleed out of me—everything I'd felt for the last year. The truth and the lies came out in that blood. Julio came out. Mickey Pesaturo came out. I knew it when I stared down at the finished tattoo.

A tall, perfect flame.

Etched into my skin forever.

I studied it in the mirror as I sat there. And I thought about the past few days. Meeting with Mickey Pesaturo changed a lot, and I'm not afraid to admit it. Today, when Shelly asked me what it's like to speak with the person you hate most, I couldn't find the right words. I don't think of Mickey Pesaturo in the same way as I did before. Little by little, I'm starting to see him as a person and not just a shadow. The badge, the gun, the uniform—it's not like that. Now when I see his face in front of me, I think of how he saw me standing on the roof of the hospital the night Julio died. He didn't run away. He didn't bail. And all this time, that's what I've been doing. Running from the truth.

I explained it to Bram when we were coming home tonight. He said he sees something different in me now, a calmness that wasn't there before. He said I found an outlet and finally turned on the light. The truth thing made him laugh. According to him, we all run from it. He does it when he looks in the mirror and then goes outside and tries to act totally white, or totally black. Same thing with Pete, Chris, Jerome and Shelly. That's how they all met in school. Running from the truth until they all found themselves standing in the same lie.

Still a lot I have to sort out. It's not something that happens overnight, and who knows what the next few days and weeks will be like. Up to me, I guess. But for now, I've got my time and my tattoo. And that's more than I've had in a long time.

4/9

I TOLD CLARE it wasn't my thing, but she dragged me to the spring dance at school tonight. After dinner, she rushed upstairs and changed into the clothes she'd bought at the thrift shop on Third Avenue. Black jeans and a bright red shirt that hugged her boobs a little too tightly. I didn't put anything special on. When we got to the auditorium, I saw a dozen freshmen standing outside, looking way too scared. Inside, there was music and a few tables of food and even a strobe light. Clare was excited, and she kept scanning the crowd for the guys she liked. Guys–plural. The girl doesn't choose them one at a time. I kept bitching about being there, but Clare said I needed a night out of the house, away from everything. I didn't believe her at first, but now I think she was right.

I found a spot on one of the bleachers and just chilled. Watched the dance floor get crowded with bodies. Then I saw him out of the corner of my eye– Josh Spindler, one of the A-list basketball players. We were in bio together last semester. He's cute. Kinda looks like Marty, with the blond hair and blue eyes, but Josh is straight. He made his way over to me and sat down. He said, "Hey, how are you?"

It started off like that, with small words and strange silent moments. I wasn't in the mood to hear his pickup lines, but believe it or not, we warmed up to each other. I'd never really noticed him before. Tonight I saw him for who he was—a cute jock who actually had a brain. He lives in the Village with his parents. Grew up in Queens and transferred to Jackson High after spending a year in private school. He told me that he'd noticed me last semester but was afraid to approach me. When I asked him why, he said, "You just never looked up from your desk. You never looked at anybody or showed interest in anything. I think I only heard your voice once." I nodded, then told him that I'd changed a little since then. We talked about our teachers and some of the students we don't like. We even talked about my life at St. Therese.

Then Josh asked me if I had a boyfriend.

The question hit me hard. I never thought anyone would ask me that again. Never thought another guy would be interested in me enough to ask me that question. I'd forgotten what it felt like to be attractive to someone.

Hesitated for a second. Looked down at my hands. Then I finally met his eyes and said, "No, I don't." He smiled and told me it was the best news he'd heard all night. Inside, I was feeling nervous and guilty—too much, moving too fast. Am I supposed to be feeling this okay about—and this ready for—new stuff? I can't help thinking Josh is cute. We only talked for about an hour, and I know I'm attracted to him. Physically, at least. He asked for my number. When I paused, he said he didn't wanna push it and gave me his instead.

I got home about twenty minutes ago. Felt so strange about the whole thing that I crumpled up the little sheet of paper with his cell number on it and chucked it into the garbage. Clare thinks I'm nuts. She collected about twenty phone numbers and plans on using each one.

It's been so long since I've had a boyfriend, or even felt that tiny sting of excitement about a guy. The last year and a half, those things never even occurred to me—love, attraction, sex. Too many emotions crowding my heart. Too much confusion. I don't know. If I see Josh again in school, I'll talk to him. For now, that's about all I can do.

10:54 P.M.

Just went back to the garbage can in the kitchen and pulled Josh's phone number from the trash. Won't hurt to keep it on file. . . .

11:30 P.M.

I hate writing about these things, these feelings. No, not feelings—urges. Sometimes they come on so strong, like when I first started dating guys back in the old neighborhood. It doesn't die, that need. And it's not just about sex. It's about feeling another person so close to you, another body wanting you and holding you. I miss that so much.

Never allowed myself to admit it, but I wanna feel that again. Maybe talking to Josh tonight woke something up inside me. Maybe he made me feel pretty. Or maybe he just reminded me that I'm still alive. That I should start living.

I'm burning up all over again, but it's a different kind of heat. And I like that I can still feel it.

4/17

HEY. BEEN A while since I last wrote. I've sorta thrown myself into school the past week, trying to finish up a few assignments I missed last month. Got an A on my English essay and I actually passed a math test. Everything else is okay. Calm, and I like that just fine. I guess the big news now is that Clare has a boyfriend. Ryan Kreshen, a sophomore. I don't know much about him, except that he calls the house every night and they talk for way too long. Yesterday he took the subway up here to our part of town. Bram met him and said he seems cool. Marty saw the guy too and thinks Clare can do better. She's spoken to me about him a few times. She seems happy. Told me that she hasn't met a guy as nice as Ryan in years.

Sitting in history class right now. Should be taking notes but it's just too boring. Only noon. The first warm sunny day and I'm locked inside. Pointless. I have two free periods after this, and then gym. I'm wondering if maybe I should get my exercise outside. . . .

2:35 P.M.

Central Park, baby! Cut out about an hour ago

and took the subway to Eighty-sixth Street and Lexington, then walked to Fifth. Feels good being here, alone. People are jogging and walking their dogs. Mothers with strollers all over the place. And cops. Lots of cops on patrol . . .

I've been thinking about him.

Mickey Pesaturo.

His face pops into my mind almost every morning when I get dressed. I look at my tattoo in the mirror, my little flame, and I remember what it stands for. Then I think back on our meeting and I hear his voice. See his face. I thought it was over when he walked out of the house that day, but it wasn't. Last night I looked at the flyer he gave me and wondered what it was all about. *Speak: A Forum for the Inner City.* For some reason he thinks I belong there. Maybe I do?

I've been afraid to mention or even think about him since we met. It's like a superstition. I made it that far, I did something good and it changed me, but what if I somehow fuck it up? I already know what Sister Ellen would say to that. She'd tell me that I'm just not used to positive things happening in my life and that I have to learn to embrace them. Or words along those lines.

Okay. Enough said. If I've learned anything, it's that I have to stop thinking and start acting. And I feel like I need to do something else. Something more. The gap between me and Mickey Pesaturo is still too big. I mean, we talked and got what we needed from each other, but what would happen if I took just one more step? What would happen if I saw him again?

4/23

SAW BRAM AND Clare after school but told them I had things to do, so instead of coming home, I set off on foot, not sure where I was headed but knowing it all the time. Braved the rain with my head hung down. One block turned into twenty, and I finally made it to the corner of West Tenth Street and Hudson. Stood there for a minute. Smoked a cigarette and stared up the block at the police precinct. White-and-blue cruisers were parked everywhere. Cops went in and came out. I swung my backpack across my shoulders and walked over to it, right into the middle of the action.

Saw everything I never wanted to see—the cops laughing and patting each other on the back, the sirens howling as new cruisers pulled up. I was okay. I was cool with it. Took a deep breath and stepped inside the precinct. Dazed and confused but handling it. A woman in uniform came up to me and asked me if I needed help. I was about to ask for Mickey Pesaturo when someone said my name.

He was standing there, behind me, eyes wide with shock.

Lost my voice for a second, then mumbled a hello.

"I'm glad to see you," he said. He was in uniform, the gun at his hip. Like on the night Julio died. He took off his cap and wiped a line of sweat from his forehead. His short hair was messy but he looked even younger this time. "Is everything okay?"

"Yeah," I said slowly, wondering. "Everything's okay." But it wasn't. I was nervous, fidgety. Started feeling like a moron but I pushed that away. Had to keep telling myself that I'd done the right thing, going to see him. I finally cleared my throat and met his eyes.

And then I thanked him, officially, for his letter and his visit. Said, "It all did a lot more for me than I probably told you when we met."

He nodded. He said he felt the same way. He told me that since our meeting, his life had changed completely. It's his hope that I start seeing everything—the cops, the inner city, myself—in a different light.

Slowly but surely, I thought. Then I reached into my backpack and pulled out the sheet of paper he'd given me the day we met. My eyes traced the words again: *Speak: A Forum for the Inner City.*

"Are you thinking about coming?" he asked.

Told him that it all depended. I asked him to tell me more about it.

"Yeah, sure." He nodded. Then he walked me over to a bank of chairs and we sat down.

He said a lot of things, but the truth is I didn't really hear much of it. I just sat next to him, kind of absorbing everything a second time. Telling myself that this was real. Happening. I was handling it.

Sitting so close to him and not freaking out, I felt stronger again. Like I knew I was moving on. Like I could face anything.

There was a pause between us, and then Mickey looked at me and asked, "How does it feel being here?"

"Strange," I told him. I took in all the movement again. The cops. It was like being in another territory, another world. The enemy's turf.

But as I looked at him and all the other cops, I realized something. Sometimes we choose our enemies, the same way we choose our friends. Our thoughts and assumptions, they're not carved in stone. Life can change quickly that way.

He said, "You haven't been in a precinct since you were arrested, right? After the riot, I mean."

Admitted that I hadn't.

"This was a big step you took," he said.

"Maybe," I answered.

"No, not maybe. I don't think most of the people you used to hang out with, the ones from your old neighborhood, would have the guts to do what you're doing. When I worked there, in the Bronx, I got nothing but grief from the teenagers. From a lot of people, actually. They looked at me, at my uniform, and that's all they'd see. It happens to most cops."

"I know," I said. "But at this point in my life, I can't speak for other people. I can't change their minds, ya know?"

"Yeah. But it's people like you who go on to change minds." He cracked a little smile. "I think you're pretty amazing, Luz."

I held his gaze for a second and then looked down at my hands. They were shaking only a little. I swear, I could've stayed there for a while, just sitting beside him and getting to know myself better. This kind of strength, I mean. Didn't know I had it in me to get past the rage and be okay . . . a *second* time.

So I agreed to go to the group meeting in a few weeks. He said I would be surprised meeting so many teenagers and different kinds of people. I guess I'm not the only one who has a gripe about the police. Not just about them, but about the politics of the department. Things like racial profiling and how so many black and Hispanic men are arrested compared to the number of whites.

I got up and told Mickey I had to go. He walked me outside, into the warm afternoon.

Before we went our separate ways, Mickey asked what made me come to the precinct today. "Was it only about the group meeting?" he asked curiously.

I answered him honestly. Shook my head and said, "No, it wasn't only for that." I looked down, then walked away. Felt his eyes following me as I headed for the subway.

4/26

EXACTLY 91 DAYS ago, I met the man who killed you. And I think he set me free.

4/28

IT WAS THE first sunny Saturday in a long time. Woke up early and let myself out of the house before Bram and Marty and Clare could see me. I walked uptown, to Hunts Point, and took the 6 train further into the Bronx.

Stared out the little windows of the train and watched the familiar sights speed by. On the street, I went past the bodega, the pizza shop, the little playground where I used to jump rope. The old neighborhood looked the same. Sad to see how messed up it still is. Broken fence, dog shit on the ground. Didn't see anyone I knew, and I was glad.

I took off on foot up Zerega Avenue. Thirty minutes later I reached St. Raymond's Cemetery. Hadn't stepped on that soil in over a year. Made my way through the rows, walking along the stones and crosses. There were so many familiar names. I'd forgotten about Billy Morales and Freddy Soto, both of them killed in a gang fight in my old neighborhood. Old Mr. Fenton worked at the gas station on Castle Hill, didn't have health insurance and died from his diabetes. I even saw Missy Gutierrez's stone. We went to grammar school together at P.S. 15, and I remember crying when I found out that she'd hanged herself in her mother's bedroom two days after her fifteenth birthday.

Julio's grave was at the far end. I stood a few feet away at first, staring. Then I went to it and knelt down. Sun in my eyes, cool wind blowing against me. I sat for a few minutes and waited. It took a while for me to believe I was really there.

I said his name. Closed my eyes and tried to remember him the way he was back when we were kids. Thought about his smile, the goofy way he used to stumble out of his bedroom and curse about everything before we went out. I saw him dead too, cold as stone, gone like yesterday.

I bought flowers from the stand outside the cemetery, and I made a little hole in the dirt beside the headstone. Pushed the stems in so that they stood up straight. One of the roses covered Julio's name. I ran my fingers along the writing, tracing back and forth over the *J*. Then I took a black marker from my backpack and scrawled my initials onto the stone. Drew a heart and a cross beside his date of birth.

It was my way of letting him know that I'd always be thinking of him. And that my going to the cemetery meant good-bye.

It was for real this time.

I felt it inside me, all the pain. I felt it slipping away.

I stared at the stone, let my hand rest on its

surface. And I knew it was time. The words kept bouncing around in my head until I let them fall, at last, from my lips.

"Julio," I whispered, "I've forgiven Mickey Pesaturo, and I forgive you too."

5/1

THIS IS HOW it was, and this is how he died:

October, a season of cool winds, rain, darkness. In the inner city, kids stare down at the streets from apartment windows and wait for their mothers to come home. Schoolyards close at dusk. There's a tight feeling in the air because people know that when the sun goes, the shooting starts early.

It was a year and a half ago. A Thursday night. I was hanging out in front of my building with Lydia and Marisol, drinking soda because none of us had enough money for beer. We shared a cigarette, listened to some music and kept our eyes on the kids playing at the curb. Lydia was saying something about needing more money when the building's front door yawned open and Julio stepped outside.

He was dressed in jeans and a padded bomber jacket. His face was tense—it had been that way for a few months. He motioned me over and said, "What you doing out here? I don't like you hanging out on the streets."

I shrugged. It was easier hanging out on the streets than at home.

"Did you eat yet?" Julio asked me.

I shook my head, then watched as he reached into his pocket and pulled out a roll of crisp cash. I saw the bills—twenties, fifties, hundreds. Like he was holding a fistful of green grass in his palm. I watched as he counted out sixty bucks and handed the money over to me.

"Here," he said. "Go buy something." He leaned down and kissed my cheek.

"Where are you going?" I asked him. But even then, I already knew.

"I'll be back." And with that, Julio disappeared down the street, got into his car and drove off.

Lydia and Marisol were happy. Sixty bucks was a fortune to us. We walked to a pizzeria a few blocks away and ate. Lydia, always innocent in her thinking, told me that I was lucky having a brother who cared about me and had so much money. I didn't say anything. My gaze found Marisol's, and her wise eyes confirmed what I had secretly known all along.

An instinct led me away from the pizzeria. I told Lydia and Marisol I had things to do, then made my way across Zerega Avenue, following it past the train station and the factories. Long blocks. Dark corners. In minutes I reached the deserted stretch of empty concrete and parking lots. It was eight o'clock. The sky was black. My heart slammed as I followed one of the alleyways around to the back of the hat factory. The forbidden area where bad shit went down. Where the body of a nineteen-year-old girl, violated and disfigured, had been discovered two years before. Where shell casings littered the ground like pebbles. I heard the voices echoing in the wind and came to a stop, then pressed myself against one of the hulking trash bins so that I'd stay hidden from view. And peering through the shadows, I saw exactly what I didn't wanna see.

Julio was standing beside his parked car, talking to a black guy. They were smoking weed. The pungent scent carried on the air as they exchanged comments, chuckled at a joke, nodded. Then Julio pulled the drugs, several tight little plastic bags, from his jacket pocket and held out his hand to the black guy. Cocaine, marijuana, heroin. Took only a second for them to complete the deal. Julio collected a wad of cash, counted it and slipped it smoothly into his pants. The black guy drove off.

The night went still. Tears thickened in my eyes as I watched Julio light a cigarette and start back to his car. It didn't surprise me. It didn't even hurt me. I cried out of frustration because I had spent too many months hoping against hope that my brother would somehow turn out differently. That he wouldn't become another neighborhood dealer building a wall of steel around himself. I cried because I knew that one day—far away, deep in the future—I would lose him to an enemy, an undercover sting, a fight gone bloody. But the end had already come.

Before Julio made it back to his car, a police cruiser sped into the parking lot, siren wailing. The red and blue lights spun wildly. They illuminated Julio's pale, panic-stricken face. He froze.

The cruiser ground to a halt. The driver's-side door popped open and a cop stepped out.

I crouched against the trash bin. *No,* I thought, *it's too soon. Give him another chance. Maybe he doesn't have any more drugs on him. Maybe his car is clean.*

The cop said, "Don't move." He held a flashlight in one hand. The other hand rested on the butt of his gun.

"Come on, man, what's your problem?" Julio said. "I can't park my car here? I'm not doing nothin' wrong."

The cop paused, then stood there and sighed. As if thinking, *We both know what you did. There's no escaping it now. Don't make this difficult.* But he said, "Turn around. Hands up and against the car."

Julio didn't move. The cigarette burned on his lips. "Why?"

"Because I said so. Hands up."

Julio threw the cigarette onto the ground. "Don't I have a right to know why?"

"This isn't a parking lot," the cop said. "It's private property and you're trespassing. Now–"

"Trespassing?" Julio shot back. "There're people in here every night. You mean to fuckin' tell me that suddenly no one's allowed?"

"Quit stalling," the cop said. "Hands up and against the car."

And for the first time, as the cruiser's white light spun out, I saw the cop's face. He was young. And the little tremor in his voice told me that he was scared. I watched, praying Julio would just do as he was told and not start any trouble.

But he had taken a step back and was inching his right hand along the side of his jacket.

The cop was quick: he slid the gun from his holster and leveled it at Julio. "Don't move," he said. And then he spoke something in code into the radio attached to his collar. He needed backup.

I bit down on my lip. My hands were shaking. As I watched, Julio took another step back. But I kept my eyes on the cop and his gun.

"A'ight," I heard Julio say. "Chill out, man. Don't make a big deal. Don't make a big deal."

And the moment sped up. It froze and shattered all in the same breath.

Something happened. It showed on the cop's face as he started and caught his breath. His hands tightened around the gun.

I saw that Julio was reaching into his waistband.

And I screamed, "No! Don't!"

In the same instant—not even a second later, no time to blink—the cop opened fire. The shot pierced the night, the vibration so loud it set off a car alarm down the street. A rat scurried out of the dark.

The bullet slammed into Julio's chest. He was blown back, his arms outstretched, his neck snapping to one side. He stood there for a few seconds, staring up at the sky like a blind man. Blood pooled in the center of his jacket. It stained his hands and dribbled from his mouth and spilled across the ground.

I ran toward him, telling myself it wasn't real. I didn't see anything but Julio. He was lying on the ground. I fell to my knees and grabbed his face and shouted his name. Sobbing. Screaming. Praying. I pushed back the jacket, gasped when I saw the hole oozing in the center of his chest. I put my hands over the wound, dipped my fingers, then both my hands, into the blood.

"Julio?" I screamed. "Julio? Please. Listen, listen to me." I stared down at his face. His lips were blue. His eyes weren't focusing.

But he spoke my name. He opened his mouth, made a sick sound, like a cough, and said, "Luz."

My hands were cradling his head. I felt the shuddering in his body, the final struggle for breath. Tears clouded my vision and I knew that it was over, that his life was slipping through my fingers and into my heart.

Beside him lay his own gun, the one I had seen in his bedroom. The one he'd gotten the day he joined his gang. The one he had probably reached for, thinking he could shoot his way out of the night.

Behind me, Mickey Pesaturo was shouting into

his police radio for backup. Voice trembling. He came to stand on the other side of Julio. There was a frightened look in his eyes. "Oh God," he was saying. "Oh Jesus. Is . . . is he okay? Is he breathing? Please—the ambulance is coming. Just another minute. Please. Oh God. Tell him to hold on. Please hold on. Jesus. Jesus."

In the distance, sirens were howling. But too late. Julio's body gave a violent final shudder and his mouth fell open.

"Is he okay?" Mickey Pesaturo said again.

I lowered Julio's shoulders onto the ground and slid my hands over his face. Then I looked up at Mickey Pesaturo. Our eyes met for the first time.

"He's dead," I whispered.

Mickey didn't move. He kept shaking his head like it wasn't true, like it couldn't be true.

And we waited there in silence—the victim, the accuser, and the accused. We waited as the wind blew and the car alarm cried out and the lights pulsed against the night sky. . . .

5:34 P.M.

And that's all I remember. After that, it's kind of blurry. But the truth isn't always clear. Sometimes we see it through smoke and have to wait until the fire dies down. Or burns up. Then it's just ashes.

This morning, I told Sister Ellen everything. Told Marty and Bram and Clare too. Wasn't easy, but I wanted them to hear it, and I wanted them to under-stand. Julio was my heart, my soul. I loved him more than anything but it was hard to accept what his life had become in the end. Like so many other young guys from the inner city, he believed that he had to battle his way through the system in order to get somewhere. And his battle was fought with guns and gangs and drugs. I tried to stop him, to protect him, but some people you just can't save. Not even your own blood.

I didn't see Julio pull his gun on Mickey Pesa-turo, but deep down inside, I know that's what hap-pened. It's happened before, to other guys from my old neighborhood who tried unloading their rage onto the cops. It's happened on every corner. Walk down any inner-city street at night and you'll hear the phantom gunshot echoing through the darkness. It's the same shot all the time. Doesn't matter if it blew someone away yesterday or ten years ago. When there's a war, everybody loses count.

Julio wasn't innocent, but his guilt is something tough to understand. His guilt was waiting to hap-pen. Growing up like he did—like we both did—had everything to do with it. When you see what we saw, hear what we heard, live the way we lived every day, life becomes a war zone. There's even a point when you stop, look up and question the difference between right and wrong. The line separating them just disappears. I was about thirteen when that happened. I think Julio was probably nine. You hungry but have no money for food? Steal. They won't hire you because they think you're a thug who can't speak English? Deal. And when the cops get in your way and don't wanna hear it, guns become your voice. You challenge the authority because the authority has already decided that you're the problem.

Nothing is black or white, but those colors matter.

I'm not making excuses for Julio. I'm just stating the facts. It's taken me this long to accept them because I was following in his footsteps, railing against the system and making the streets my home. For so long, Mickey Pesaturo was the enemy, and everything he represented angered me. I'll always wish he hadn't pulled that trigger. But to go on hating him and believing that my kind can't get along with his kind is pointless. I can still fight for what I believe in. I just can't lose myself in the process.

Finding your own strength and knowing it's true. Walking on common ground but still rising above it. Maybe that's justice?

6/13

SUMMER IN THE city: crowded streets, vicious heat, and the sky like shrapnel, steely gray. I move quickly through the days and chill at night. Sometimes I sit on the front stoop watching the traffic buzz by on 135th Street, listening as Bram cuts the noise with his guitar. It's his new instrument. Taught himself how to play about a month ago and he's sounding good. When it rains, I sit in Clare's room—she's still dating Ryan—and pretend to be interested in her outfits as she tries them on again and again. Marty always needs help with his flyers for the GLBTU club he started at school. If I feel like drawing, I crash with him in the living room, and together we create cool little designs that always seem to spark controversy. Last week we did a sketch of two people kissing, both of them with short hair and similar features—two guys? Two girls? A guy and a girl? All leads to the same place, if you ask me. We're both members of the AVTF (Antiviolence Task Force), and once a week the club meets in the auditorium to talk about our safety and how we can stop getting hurt and stop hurting each other. Don't know if it'll work, but I'm trying.

A month and a half gone by since I last wrote.

Feels like forever. Feels like yesterday. All in all, it feels okay. Haven't thought about writing because I've been wired up, doing a million things. School's almost done. College applications to fill out. Guess I got lost in the craziness of it all.

Check this: Sister Ellen asked me if I had any plans tonight. We were in her office, right in the middle of one of our Twisted Sister sessions, when she brought it up. She saw the flyer on my desk. I haven't moved it since Mickey Pesaturo gave it to me. Told her I felt strong enough to do just about anything, and she smirked and thanked God for the "blessed rage" of the last year.

I hear that. And I understand what she means. Blessed rage=blessed release.

Back in May, I met up with Anne Burns and filed my official statement with the courts about what happened the night Julio died. And because of that, Mickey Pesaturo is patrolling the streets again, a cop with a regular beat. I'm calm with it. He's at peace too. Plus, my probation sentence was lifted.

Sitting at my desk now, staring at the flyer. It's six o'clock and light out. I've got somewhere to be.

11:25 P.M.

A forum for the inner city. That's what the flyer said. That's what the sign on the door said. The room was full when I walked in. At least fifty people were gathered in a circle of chairs–black, white,

Hispanic, Cuban, Asian. Mothers and fathers. Men in business suits. Even teenagers my own age. There were five community relations officers manning the door, and they acted cool and polite, asking me if I wanted water or soda. I shook my head and stood on the threshold for a minute, looking around. No familiar faces, until I saw Mickey Pesaturo.

He came over to me and we shook hands. He was in uniform. "I'm really glad you came," he said. "I was afraid maybe you wouldn't."

Asked him why he thought that.

He didn't answer at first. He stood there and considered, not meeting my eyes. "Because I was just afraid you wouldn't," he finally said. "After all you've been through, after these past couple of months . . ."

I looked him in the eyes, straight up. It was easy this time. No bullshit between us. No fake words. I said, "I'm handling it. And I came because I wanted to. For me."

He nodded. Understood. We sat down in the chairs and talked about what'd been going on in the city the past couple of weeks. There had been three more police brutality cases filed, and all of them had made the news. Two of the victims were young, in their twenties. One black, the other Puerto Rican. Both claimed to have been roughed up by cops. The third was a middle-aged white woman who told reporters that she was handcuffed and kicked in the face by a cop after she yelled at him. A routine traffic stop, but it ended in violence.

I asked Mickey what he thought about those cases.

"An investigation on one of them has been completed, and I think we're gonna see that the arresting officer was out of line," he said. "It'll be mentioned tonight."

And it was. Along with a million other issues.

The meeting started with a speech from a lieutenant, an Irishman who's retired now. McCormick, I think his name was. Grew up in Queens in a white neighborhood, but now those streets are considered low income and "at risk." He talked about working that beat and about how, no matter what he said or did, the black teenagers refused to trust him. He tried to help. He tried to play his part in bettering the community. But the stone wall had already been built too high. The people in that neighborhood looked at him and saw an enemy.

Other cops stood up and talked about the same thing. All their experiences on the streets, how the white ones had to work harder to get even a tiny bit of respect. Minority police officers spoke up too. One, a woman cop whose name was Ramirez, said she didn't understand why her own people—Hispanics—looked at her as if she'd traded in her identity for a badge. She got shit on when she walked the streets in uniform. Why, when she was only trying to protect and serve?

I sat there and listened to all the responses. The teenagers in the front row, maybe ten of them, were vocal about everything. They stood up and posed their own questions. Why did they get hassled for hanging out on the corners? Why were they always subjected to random searches for no reason? When one of them got scared and ran from the cops, why was he chased down like an animal and subdued with nightsticks? White cops. Black and Hispanic civilians. Why couldn't they mix? Voices got loud in the room, and three of the older women started crying. They were clutching pictures of young men. In memoriam.

There was another side to the room, though. People who'd had different experiences and understood why the cops had to act like they did spoke their minds. A black guy stood in the middle of the floor with his young kids and said that it was the job of the people to ease all the tensions. Up to us, he said, because the cops don't know who to trust. We have to show them respect in order to receive it. He said, "Those of us who live in the inner city don't mind giving respect to each other or even to some of the thugs who keep us awake at night. But we're not willing to treat police officers the same way. The picture just ain't right."

I was glad to hear someone say it. Back in my old neighborhood, I was guilty of respecting almost everybody except authority figures. Cops came around and I'd spit on the ground. My friends acted the same way. Julio always got respect, even though people knew he was in a gang and dealing drugs.

The point? Sometimes we create our own battles.

Toward the end of the night, everybody gathered in a circle for a prayer service. Candles were handed out. Lights went down. The room glowed with a quiet softness as a minister asked God to remember all those lost to the streets. Then came the roll call. A dozen names were read aloud, names of young people who'd died as a result of justified force . . . and names of officers who'd gone down in the line of duty while trying to protect the streets. When it was his turn to speak, Mickey Pesaturo held out a candle and said, "Julio Cordero. Rest in peace."

I stared at him. The candlelight lit his face. The room went silent and I felt, suddenly, like it was just the two of us standing there. I thought my mind would automatically bring us back to that night over a year ago, but nothing about the moment changed. He came over to me and put the candle in my hands. Our fingers brushed together. Then his eyes glassed over and the emotion hit me too. I cried. We both did. We stood there until the room emptied out and the last bit of confusion left me.

I let him walk me out of the precinct. On the

street, he asked me if I was gonna be okay. Told him I'd be fine. Then his radio started crackling and a cruiser pulled up, lights flashing. He had to respond to a call.

"Get home safe," he said.

"You too." I watched as he got into the cruiser and drove off.

The sirens blared in the distance. Made me think about the people I listened to tonight, the cops and the regular folk, the teenagers. Words. Stories. Tears. In the beginning they might not mean anything, but when they start falling into place, it's the darkness that burns up, the fear that things will never change. And sometimes, they do.

I turned and looked up. Bram, Marty and Clare were waiting at the corner, standing there in a tight little knot. Bodies stiff. Eyes wide but hopeful. I went up to them and asked how long they'd been hanging out.

"A while," Bram said. "In case you needed us." He lit a cigarette and passed it to me.

I shook my head. Another cruiser came screaming down the street as pedestrians pushed back onto the sidewalks. It was the usual chaos of nighttime in the city.

"There was a shooting uptown," Clare said, as if reading my mind. "The traffic is really bad."

Marty shrugged. "Whatever. Let's start back. Sister Ellen said we have a group meeting later."

Bram linked his arm through mine. The night was clear, and the steady stream of police cruisers lit the streets in red and blue. I didn't look back. I rested my head on Bram's shoulder as Marty and Clare led the way.

We followed the sirens home.

STATISTICS

- Of the 1.8 million children in New York City, it is estimated that approximately 450,000 come into contact with the child welfare system at some point.

  —New York City Administration for Children's Services

- Parental substance abuse is often a factor in cases in which children are placed in foster care. Currently, there are about 24,500 children in foster care in New York City.

  —New York City Administration for Children's Services

- In 2002, 3,012 children and teens lost their lives to gun violence. That's 8 children and teens per day.

  —The Brady Center to Prevent Gun Violence

- In 2001, 79 percent of homicide victims ages ten to twenty-four were killed with firearms.

  —Centers for Disease Control and Prevention

FOR ADDITIONAL INFORMATION, PLEASE CONTACT:

The Brady Center to Prevent Gun Violence
202-289-7319
www.bradycenter.org

National Youth Violence Prevention
Resource Center
866-SAFEYOUTH
(866-723-3968)
www.safeyouth.org

Teens, Crime, and the Community
c/o National Crime Prevention Council
202-466-6272
www.nationaltcc.org

ANTONIO PAGLIARULO was born in Manhattan and raised in the Bronx. He attended Fiorello H. LaGuardia High School of Music & Art and Performing Arts, and Purchase College, State University of New York, where he earned a BA in sociology. He has written about crime, entertainment, and spirituality for numerous publications. He has also worked as a tutor for inner-city teenagers.

Antonio Pagliarulo lives in New York City.